The Days of Joseph

JOHN NOBLE

Cover Produced by Damonza

Editing by Carol Noble

For Rachel, the little one in the family who always wears a smile

Contents

Chapter 1
Moreh

Canaan
1900 BC
The Grove of Oracles

Dinah hesitated a moment outside the ring of low-hanging terebinth trees.

"Come on!" Isnah glanced back with a grin as a gust of wind whipped her long skirt against her legs. "It's just through here." She ducked down into a gap between the thick bush-like trees and vanished behind the wall of green terebinth leaves.

Past the foliage, Dinah could hear drifting voices, the noise of laughter and merriment. Still though, she couldn't avoid a spike of nervousness. She glanced over at Amaleigh, her gaze lingering a moment on the other girl's smooth linen gown, embroidered with little white roses on a field of red. Next to her friends, Dinah felt very out of place in her mom's thick yellow dress, even after the struggle she'd been through the last two days getting it fitted to her slim figure.

Dinah bit at her lower lip. "Are you sure that–"

"Oh, just come on." Amaleigh took her hand and tugged her towards the wall of trees and twigs. "You look fine. Besides, Isnah said we'd have a good time. You can't do that from out here."

Dinah stooped and found herself in a tunnel of shadowed jade, leaves and twigs brushing at her shawl.

Suddenly they were through, and she found herself standing amid a swirl of people.

The clearing formed a wide, grassy circle. Despite the breeze outside, the air within hung still and heavy with the pine sweet scent of incense. In the center towered an ancient oak, with a gnarled trunk thicker than she was tall and broad branches that sprawled out in every direction. The lowest drooped towards the ground like the sagging arms of an exhausted giant, his hands gloved in vibrant greenery.

It was majestic and… a little unnerving at the same time. She'd seen it often from afar, but up close, more than anything, the oak reminded Dinah of an old man with a half dozen freakishly long arms.

Everyone else seemed perfectly at ease though, and she and her friends appeared to be the last of the wedding party to arrive. The clearing was swarming with men wearing the long tan robes and red shoulder sashes so popular in town, while women strutted about in a rainbow of gorgeous *šaddīnu* dresses and shawls. Meanwhile, most of the younger girls like Isnah wore simple dresses with the sky blue, virgin's sash around their waist.

Over at the base of the oak, the happy couple stood surrounded by an eager crowd, the smoke from their incense spiraling higher in a hazy tendril. Apparently, burning puffs of incense to the sacred tree was *the thing* to do. Isnah was already halfway over, and Amaleigh spent a moment prodding at Dinah. "Come on, they say if you burn a leaf from the tree with your incense and breathe it in, you breathe in a bit of the wisdom of the ancients."

Dinah hesitated a second, "You sure about that?" Her skeptical eyes followed Isnah, as she went about delicately preparing her own incense tray.

Amaleigh followed her gaze. "Oh, Isnah doesn't really count," she scoffed. "She wastes her time trying to figure out who her future husband is, which… "

Amaleigh grinned, rolling her eyes in exasperation. "Well, let's not go there again."

Yes, *let's not*, Dinah found herself silently nodding in agreement.

"You really should burn a pinch of incense," Amaleigh continued. "For luck if nothing else. I'm not sure what the point of coming is if you don't."

"I'm… fine, really," Dinah insisted. Truthfully, she knew her mom and dad wouldn't have approved, if they heard about it. Her family worshipped their own God.

She still remembered when she'd been maybe five and they'd come from Harran. They had met… well, everyone called them messengers, sent by the God her family followed. Tall men with burnished armor and fine woven tunics so white they seemed to glow in the sun. One of them had caught her favorite blanket when the wind whipped it out of her nervous hands. All these years later, she still distinctly remembered his face when he'd leaned down to return it — buoyant, bright-eyed and friendly. Like they could be best friends even though they'd never met and he was twice her height. It was weird, but she… she didn't feel like he'd want her burning incense to the tree. "Just, you go, Amaleigh."

Dinah's friend gave an exaggerated huff. "Suit yourself."

She tromped off towards Isnah, leaving Dinah shuffling her feet a moment, a little unsure what to do. Eventually she settled on just wandering the edge of the grove, admiring the terebinth trees, now fruiting and sprouting long stems speckled with tiny scarlet berries. Picking one, she admired it for a moment, like a cluster of rosy grapes…

"You know you're not supposed to pick those." A masculine voice cut into her musings.

She spun to find a young man a few paces away – tall, with a familiar face, tasteful clothes and short cropped dark hair done up in a tight knot, the new style in town. An amused grin danced on his confident features. "They say it's bad luck to pick the terebinth fruits before they're ripe." He nodded to the one in her hand.

Dinah blushed, modestly tugging her shawl up over her head as she dipped in a polite curtsy, "Shechem." They weren't exactly close acquaintances, but she'd been around enough to at least recognize the prince of the city, King Hamor's oldest son, Amaleigh's third cousin and Isnah's first.

"Dinah–*bat*–Jacob." Shechem used her formal name, Dinah daughter of Jacob. The same way she'd introduced herself when they'd first met months ago. His deliberate tone, almost savoring the words, left her vaguely wondering if he was making fun of her. "Call me mad, but for some reason, I didn't expect to see you here."

Oh, he certainly wasn't mad. Entirely too handsome, painfully arrogant, frequently crass, and far too enamored with himself, but not mad.

Before she could summon up a pithy retort, Shechem kept right on talking. "I noticed you seem to have forgotten your incense. I thought I might offer you a pinch."

That was… a bit of a surprise. In her limited experience, Shechem typically didn't notice anyone outside himself.

"I'm fine," she nodded.

He glanced towards the berries still in her hand. "Except for the bad luck from picking that."

Dinah flicked the cluster of berries away. "And how is an oak supposed to help?"

"Oh, Moreh is more than just an oak," Shechem said, with a hint of grandeur in his tone. "It's the place of Ba'al Berith, the lord of the promise. That's why married couples come here to burn incense as a part of their vows. It's a place of wisdom and guidance for the future."

Dinah still wasn't fully convinced. She glanced over to where her friends were still making their supplications. "All that from an oak tree?"

"Of course," he nodded and met her eyes with an oddly pleasant smile. "Your father has that altar up on the mountainside. I thought your family did the same thing?"

Well, she mused, they did… sometimes. When she'd been little they'd made offerings pretty regularly, lately though they certainly weren't as diligent about it as Shechem's people seemed to be. Admittedly, her dad did seem to genuinely care, but…

Suffice to say it was complicated in her family. Certainly not something she wanted to talk about, even if Shechem was oddly *not* being a jerk for once.

Thankfully he wasn't waiting around to listen. "Speaking of family," Shechem said, cheerful, "I haven't seen any of your usual bodyguards lurking around today. I'm surprised they let you come alone."

He probably didn't mean much by it, but Dinah felt a twinge of annoyance at the remark. There were some definite perks to being the little sister of the family, but having a half dozen older brothers hawking over her shoulder whenever she went to see her friends wasn't one of them.

"They're watching the herds," she said curtly. "Besides, Reuben and Simeon don't run my life."

"Of course not," Shechem agreed, a smirk tugging at his face. "I'm sure they're too busy sleeping with the sheep to bother," he added, chuckling to himself as though it were a grand joke.

Crude at it was, it took Dinah a heartbeat to grasp the 'humor' in Shechem's insinuation about her brothers. When she did though her expression instantly soured. There was the Shechem they all knew and… well, didn't really like *at all*.

"You know what," she glanced over to where her friends were still busy and made a snap decision, "it was a beautiful wedding, but I'm done." She added frostily, "Why don't you go back to sniffing your tree."

With that she wheeled and stalked off, making for the grove entrance. She hadn't gone more than ten steps when she heard Shechem's voice behind her, suddenly apologetic. "Dinah, wait."

"What?" she snapped, not even looking back. "You have some more snide insults you've been saving?"

Dinah reached the little green tunnel that marked the entrance to the grove and ducked down, her shawl still pulled over her head as she forced her way past the gauntlet of twigs and leaves. She hoped he might just give up and leave her alone, but she could hear the rustle of him following. When she emerged into the open, he was only a few steps behind. "Dinah, I'm sorry."

She spun back to fix him with a withering glare. "No you're not," she said, disgusted. "Since when have you been sorry about anything?"

"I–"

"Why do you even care anyway?"

For a moment Shechem didn't answer, instead he stood there, just… staring at her. But not at her eyes. Instead his gaze drifted lower, lingering at her chest, and leaving her with an unsettling sense in her gut, like a dream where she'd forgotten to wear her clothes. Her hands unconsciously fell to her side, clutching at her skirt, like she needed the reassurance that it was still there.

Shechem spoke, his voice more subdued. "That's a very pretty sash." He nodded to the hand-width strip of teal blue linen tied around her waist.

"Well, you should go tell Amaleigh," Dinah said, suddenly wishing she *did* have one of her brothers around. "I borrowed it from her."

"Is she still finished with boys and sworn to spinsterhood?" Shechem grinned like he was trying to lighten the mood.

"Why don't you go ask," Dinah said, sarcastic. She turned to leave, muttering, "I'm starting to think she has a point."

Then a hand closed around her wrist. "Wait," Shechem insisted.

She looked back, her eyes narrowing. *No one* grabbed her like that. Shechem was three years her elder, with a lithe build and about forty pounds on her, most of it muscle, but she was a daughter of Jacob, and around here that meant something. Her voice was slow, deliberate, and ice cold. "*Don't* – touch me."

She tried to jerk her wrist free, but Shechem's grip tightened like a vise. Dinah felt a swell of anger mingled with dread.

"Let go," she snapped, fire in her voice, even as he roughly dragged her a step closer. He didn't stop.

"Shechem!" Her voice grew sharp and desperate as he leaned in like he was trying to kiss her. She turned her head and frantically tried to wrench herself away, "Shechem! Let me go!" Panic stabbed at her chest as he dragged her close, and a hand closed over her mouth as she tried to scream. "Let me–"

Chapter 2
The Youngest Brother

4 Days Later

Joseph was glad to be back in camp, even if it was for bad news. There was just something profoundly unfulfilling about being trapped out in the fields and sleeping all night with the herd. The grass was supposed to be soft and springy, but after about an hour tossing in the dark, it always felt hard as a rock.

And then, of course, there was the company, which was sorely lacking. Really, it was like some of his brothers thought being out in the field was an excuse to act like animals too. They always came up with the stupidest games to while the hours away. A little optimistic voice in the back of his head piped up, could be worse. At least he was getting pretty good at fighting with his staff.

Except that all his brothers were just as good, Joseph mused glumly, plus they were bigger and stronger. Turned out that brawn, in sufficient quantities, did tend to triumph over brain, and Joseph had the welts to prove it. He sighed, trying to push the depressing thought aside. At least he was back home. He breathed in the familiar smells − goat leather, smoking lamb, spicy stew, and of course, cheese, lots of cheese. Together they could get a bit tangy at times, but it was still the camp. Things were always better in the camp.

The scores of tents were pitched in a wide circle, with an open area in the center that was the closest thing they had to a market square. When they'd first come to Canaan, years ago, their camp had been a thin ring of tents nestled down the valley from the city. Since then, the circle had thickened as the encampment gradually grew into something akin to a bustling, miniature town.

Making his way along the inner ring of the sprawling camp, Joseph passed several servants scurrying around the cook tent, a low hung, goatskin canvas that stretched back a good twenty feet with both the front and back open to let the air through. It was wafting good smells today– yeasty fresh bread, honey and a whole battery of spices. What looked like an entire lamb was slow roasting over a firepit behind. A few servant girls, Tamarra, Fannah, and Remmi, were sitting idly under the awning, chatting in hushed whispers and pretending to be crushing grain into flour if anyone looked.

A few older ladies were busy preparing the dough. Meanwhile, most of the actual cooking was being done by the resident camp master chef, a dark tan man from a river land far east of Ur, who everyone just called Dhra. He made fantastic sweet bread with honeyed fruit and steaming pies with seasoned goose stuffed inside.

Normally, he was too wrapped up in experimenting to pay much attention, and Joseph could have swiped a round loaf of bread to tide him over until dinner. But today, Dhra was busy laying out dish after savory dish on a wide cloth while Bilhah and Zilpah, his dad's third and fourth wives, were busying themselves arranging everything just so. It looked like they were about to have a feast, although given the circumstances, he couldn't fathom why.

Nevertheless, with Zilpah hawking around, Joseph didn't bother trying to get something to eat. If she noticed him, she'd just chase him off anyway. Instead, he left Dhra to whatever banquet he was preparing. Strolling around the circular camp, Joseph aimed for a smaller tent situated next to the impressively tall, almost palatial awning where his dad received guests.

Typically, the entire front of the meeting tent was kept opened to the outside. Without a breeze it tended to get stuffy, especially beneath the blazing noon sun. Today though, it was closed up, the entire front walled off by a thick layer of canvas that veiled whatever was happening inside.

Something was going on. Off to the side three horses stood with heavy riding blankets draped across their backs. Their reins were tied to a post where they waited, anxiously pawing at the dirt.

It wasn't every day you saw one of those, let alone three. Especially not here.

Horses meant somebody important. Most merchants from the desert used camels and outside of one *very* wealthy Hattian, Joseph had never seen just a random traveler on a horse. So… likely from Shechem? That narrowed the list down to, well, basically Hamor or one of his sons. Possibly one of Hamor's captains, but with three horses, probably Hamor himself and a couple of his lieutenants.

That was bold, showing his face around here after what had happened. The message they'd gotten hadn't detailed the whole story, but it was enough and…

Joseph stared a moment before finally quashing down his curiosity. Whatever it was that Hamor wanted, Joseph knew Dad would probably tell him later anyway. For the moment, he had someone else he needed to see first.

Turning to the smaller tent off to the right, Joseph strolled over, waiting a second by the curtain flap at the voices inside. "Mom? Are you there?"

"Joseph?" His mother's voice came back surprised, but lighthearted and happy. She'd been that way a lot lately. "Just a minute," she called out.

Joseph heard the rustle of cloth inside the tent, along with another, slightly accented but familiar woman's voice. A moment later his mom called again, "Come in, Joseph."

He stooped a little to push aside the white curtain flap, and a hint of lavender mingled with the sweet aroma of cedar greeted him. His mom always had a little block of fresh cedar wood lying about to 'liven up the place'. Compared to the reeking tang of sweat, hide, poop, and grass that he'd been living in, it smelled an awful lot like home.

Out in the field, the best he could hope for was a simple lean-to with a cloth thrown over the top. His mom's tent though, was more like a house with walls made of goat leather. Light spilled in from windows screened with white cotton that let the breeze through while keeping out the dust. The tent laid out into a square room, supported by cedar poles with the thickest holding up a peak in the center. Even the dirt floor was carpeted over with colorful seating cushions and beige flaxen mats.

Joseph found three women inside. His mom was sitting near the center of the room, while Althea and her daughter Myrrha crowded around. Althea was a little younger than his mom, although her plain face creased with crow's feet made her look older. Myrrha was Joseph's age, slim, with chestnut hair and cream white skin.

Althea had her hand on his mom's pregnant belly, which had gone from a pronounced bump the last time Joseph had seen her, to a swollen stomach like she'd strapped on a cushion beneath her gown. "You haven't felt any tightness since?" Althea was asking, her back to the entrance.

"No, and it was just for a few heartbeats, then it stopped," his mom explained. "I wasn't sure if I should mention it but…"

Althea nodded, "You did the right thing."

His mom seemed to relax some, and her eyes turned to Joseph, a smile lighting up her delicate features.

"Hey, Mom." Joseph got the sense he was intruding, "I can come back later if you were–"

"No, no," she cheerfully gestured him over, "You're back. How was it?"

How was spending three weeks herding a bunch of unruly animals? It was… smelly, exhausting, miserable, more than a little disgusting sometimes… Joseph sighed, "It was hot." He settled for the least objectionable description. "We didn't lose any lambs though."

"That's good," his mom nodded. "I'm glad it went well."

"Yeah," Joseph mumbled half-heartedly. That wasn't really how he would have described the experience, but he shoved that aside. "How's the baby?"

"He's…" his mom took a half second to settle on a word, "active. He's been kicking on and off all morning."

Mom tapped at her belly, almost like she was trying to get the baby's attention, even as she gestured him closer. He'd seen her talking to the baby before, which was doubly weird. "That's your big brother. His name's Joseph," Mom said to the baby with a wide grin.

Joseph wasn't sure if the baby could hear her, but… maybe it had. The possibility was enough to finally draw a real smile to his face.

When he looked up from his mom's baby-bump though, he noticed her smile had dimmed and she was staring at his face, a hint of worry in her eyes. "Joseph, what happened to your cheek?"

Oh… that.

His hand unconsciously strayed to the painful bruise below his right eye. He'd been thinking Mom might not notice. His face was already smudged with dirt and hadn't looked that bad yesterday. Granted, he'd been checking his reflection in a stream, not the best mirror, so… yeah.

"Joseph, what happened?" His mom touched the bruise, and Joseph tried not to wince at her probing.

"It's nothing," he mumbled. "Just an accident."

"An accident?" He caught skepticism in his mom's voice and tried to look anywhere else. His eyes fell on Myrrha. She was standing off to the side, quiet and demure, but Joseph still caught her sarcastic eye roll at his words.

"We were just playing around and…" His voice trailed off halfway through his excuse, and his mom fixed him with a glare. "It was an accident."

For a heartbeat Joseph felt a tightness in his gut at the possibility that his mom might not let it drop, that she might make a stink about it. Again.

A few years back he'd showed up with a black eye and she'd lost it. She'd stormed over to her sister's tent and the two had ended up in a shouting match over grudges that were older than he was. Somehow his dad had gotten involved, and by the time all was said and done, what actually *had* been a sparring accident between him and Zebulun had turned into a mess like a pile of goat droppings in the tent. Of course, it hadn't fixed anything either, mostly just made it worse.

That was back then though. Back when he was younger, and Mom wasn't eight months pregnant. When he dared to meet her glare for a second, he caught frustration in her eyes. But after a moment she nodded, even if she didn't look happy about it. "You're sure?"

"Yes," Joseph nodded with a twinge of relief.

His mother let out a heavy sigh, and Joseph glanced at Althea, who served as the resident camp midwife before looking back to his mom. "Is everything ok with the baby?"

"It's fine," she nodded, reassuringly. "Just your little brother eager to get out."

Joseph didn't know enough to disagree with the diagnosis, "Okay, I've got some stuff to do so…" He didn't finish the sentence so much as stand to leave.

Mom smiled. "I'm glad to have you back, Joseph."

Joseph stooped and swept aside the tent flap to go. Outside though, he hesitated. A part of him was still curious if things were okay with his new baby – he didn't want to say baby *brother* just yet. It felt silly, but he didn't want to jinx things.

The tent didn't stop noise very well, and inside he could hear Althea's slight Achaean accent. "Okay, Rachel, I want you to lie back and just breathe… there you go. We need to make sure your womb is nice and relaxed for when the baby comes, so I'll give it a massage, very gentle. Tell me if anything hurts or tickles, alright?"

Joseph gave a mental shrug. That didn't sound too bad. He started walking, heading for somewhere to wash off, but hadn't gotten more than two dozen steps when he heard sandaled feet behind. He turned to see Myrrha jogging to catch up and looking oddly happy for carrying a clay chamber pot in her arms.

"Hey, Joseph." She slowed to match his pace.

Joseph eyed the lidded chamber pot skeptically. "Hey." They'd been friends for a long time, but running off with his mom's toilet pot was… "They have you scrubbing the privy pots again?"

"Oh this?" An impish grin slid onto Myrrha's face. "I was just heading over to go dump it on top of the witc…" She glanced around and caught herself mid-word when she noticed Issachar and Zebulun not too far away, talking in quiet whispers.

Joseph held back a snort of laughter. His dad's first wife had always struck him as bitter, creepy-eyed, and well… witchy.

Unfortunately, calling her that in front of her two youngest boys was just a quick way to start another fight, probably earn Myrrha a beating, and end with

14

both of them scrubbing chamber pots. The mental image was still pretty hilarious though.

He asked, "Seriously, what're you doing with that thing?"

Myrrha shrugged, "Mom wanted me to take it. You can use it to tell if someone has problems. She shows me sometimes."

Joseph cringed. "That sounds like a dirty job."

Myrrha leaned a bit closer with a smirk and sniffed at his clothes, wrinkling her nose at the concentrated smell of three weeks working with animals. "You're one to talk, stinky."

She elbowed him, good-naturedly, but Joseph drew a sharp hiss at the spike of pain when she nudged his ribs.

Instantly all the playfulness vanished from Myrrha's voice, replaced with worried concern. "Are you okay?"

"I'm fine." He brushed it off.

From the skepticism on her face Myrrha didn't believe a word of it. "That's *siliāti* and you know it." She sighed and folded her arms, her face serious. "Can I take a look?"

Joseph didn't agree, but he didn't stop her either, and they'd been friends long enough for that to count as a yes. The two ducked behind the nearest tent, and setting the chamber pot aside, Myrrha gently lifted his tunic. Joseph saw her face crease in shock and worry when she viewed the purplish welts on his side. "Joseph, what happened?"

She let his tunic drop but fixed him with a razor glare.

Joseph let out a long breath, "It was just a… a…"

"A what?" she demanded, angry, and more than a little sarcastic. "An accident? Your mom may buy that, but don't expect–"

"Okay, my cheek *was* an accident," Joseph snapped, thumbing towards the bruise beneath his eye.

In a way that was all the answer Myrrha needed. For a moment the two just stood there, Joseph's breaths heavy and angry while Myrrha just looked sad, her eyes downcast.

Finally, Myrrha let out a frustrated sigh, walked back over, and picked up the chamber pot. "Well, come on." She started out for her and her mother's tent.

"Huh?"

"Somebody has to patch you up," she pointed out in a practical tone.

"Myrrha, I'm okay."

"*Obviously* not." She gave an exaggerated eye-roll. "Joseph, if your mom knew I'd seen that and hadn't helped, she'd have my hide. *My mom* would have my hide. So… please, just let me help."

Joseph didn't say okay, but he didn't say no either, and they'd been friends long enough for that to count as a yes.

Chapter 3
Myrrha

"What are you making?" Joseph couldn't help but peer over at Myrrha as she busied herself with a small knife, peeling the pale green skin off a thick, serrated aloe branch that looked like all the fleshy prickliness of a cactus, crossed with the shape of a long, narrow fern leaf.

"This should help," Myrrha said absently, as she focused on her work.

She'd pulled the whole front curtain aside, converting the stuffy tent to an open-fronted room that looked out across the camp while still offering some wonderfully cool shade. Now the two sat cross-legged on the woven flax floor mat.

Unlike the comparatively lavish quarters his family enjoyed, Myrrha's place was fairly humble, a small tent with enough room for two bedrolls, some clay pots, and a few reed baskets filled with sewing tools, bandages or just a change of clothes. As bond servants they didn't own much, but in camp a lot of things were shared, so they'd always gotten by.

But if the inside of their tent was cramped and spartan, the front was a sort of mad apothecary's lair. Herbs hung on sticks in tight bundles to slow dry in the scorching sun. Out front sat a jumble of exotic looking greenery in clay pots that Myrrha always complained about having to fetch water for. On the side of the tent, a little vegetable garden that sprouted the occasional scented flower in spring rounded out the feel.

Joseph had picked up a few of the herb names over the years– lavender, thyme, oregano, and one with little black berries that he was pretty certain was deadly poisonous nightshade. He wasn't sure why they kept that around.

Regardless, Joseph was starving, and the oregano was something spicy to nibble on, so while Myrrha worked, he set about stripping a thin oregano stalk, pinching off one leaf at a time.

Myrrha's tent was about a quarter way around the circular camp, a kind of middling position in the camp hierarchy, but it did offer a decent view of his dad's tent, the horses still impatiently stamping around out front.

"Any idea what's going on over there?" he asked after a few moments.

The question was enough to finally drag Myrrha out of her work, and she glanced up for a heartbeat, following his gaze. "Hamor," she said without much elaboration, "and I think he brought some of his goon cousins along."

"Well, I could guess that," Joseph said, "but why is he here after… well…?"

Joseph didn't finish but Myrrha seemed to get his meaning. She shot him a side glance, her voice turning quiet. "What all did you hear?"

"Not a lot," he said, "but something about Hamor kidnapping Dinah."

Dinah was Joseph's older half-sister, by his dad's first wife, Leah. Leah was also, incidentally, Joseph's mom's sister, which made life even more confusing. Especially since the two had a long simmering feud over if Leah was even supposed to be married to his dad in the first place.

Anyway, by Joseph's reckoning, that made Dinah something like his three-quarters sister from the opposite end of their four-sided chaos family. That said, she'd always been a lot nicer than her older brothers, a bit of a princess sometimes, but otherwise Joseph liked to think they'd at least been on good terms. All the rumors swirling about had left a cold lump in his stomach.

"What exactly happened?" he asked. The message they'd gotten out in the field had sounded bad, and a part of him was hoping that maybe there had been something lost along the way.

"Well, I haven't heard that much," Myrrha said quietly. That was, of course, nonsense. Rumors got around camp about as fast as you could walk, and Joseph knew she'd been a lot closer with Dinah than he had. "It was four days ago," Myrrha said, "She went into town with umm… you remember Amaleigh and Isnah? The girls with all the henna designs on their arms."

"Vaguely." The names sounded familiar and Joseph felt like he'd seen them around. "Hamor's cousins… or something? Right?" He felt like the whole town of Shechem was interrelated in one mind-bending way or another.

"I think Isnah may be his first cousin's daughter, but yeah," Myrrha nodded. "She went to see them. I think someone in town was getting married. Anyway," Myrrha's expression turned grim, "I've heard it a few different ways, but the short of it is that Shechem kidnapped and he… he raped her. No one's seen Dinah since."

Joseph felt like his heart had dropped straight to his gut. So, it was true.

Shechem, confusingly named after the city his father ruled, was Hamor's first son and future heir to the city of Shechem, situated a couple miles up the valley from their camp. He wasn't exactly known as a paragon of virtue, but even so, he wouldn't just kidnap…

Joseph muttered a low curse, a stab of anger in his voice. "No one stopped him?"

She went back to crushing the thick aloe leaf with her mortar and pestle, picking out the green husks left behind. "Well, his dad is in charge and…" Her voice trailed off and she just left it with a simple shrug.

"So that means he can do whatever he wants?"

Myrrha didn't bother with an answer, she just busied herself grinding away. They both knew that was *exactly* what it meant.

Joseph felt the frustration boiling over. He picked another tiny leaf off the oregano, but instead of eating it he flung it away. The speck of green fluttered an unsatisfyingly short distance. "I can't believe no one stopped him."

For a moment there was just silence, but at last, "I can," Myrrha said in a small voice.

Joseph glanced over at her, confusion written on his face, "How so?"

Myrrha hesitated an instant, like she didn't know if she should say more. "I've been going to town sometimes with Samas," she explained, still staring down at the crushed aloe, "mostly to buy herbs or linen bandages, and from the looks I get from people on the street…" She shivered despite the heat. "I wouldn't go there alone."

Joseph had to think on that for a moment, even as he tried to piece out what all that meant, for them… the camp… everyone. If it had been one of the servants, someone like… well, like Myrrha, they probably could have settled things, but Dinah was a whole different basket of eggs.

Hamor being here meant he was trying to reach an accommodation. Even so, after what Shechem had done? Joseph wasn't sure what sort of bride price would fix that.

Next to him Myrrha pulled over a small wooden chest and twisted her body around like she was trying to hide whatever was in it. With the front tent flap pulled away, anyone who wandered by could see inside.

Joseph found himself peering after her as she opened the wooden chest to reveal an interior packed with straw, from which she delicately pulled out a small bottle of translucent bluish glass.

Joseph blinked in surprise. Wow, that was rare. He'd seen a few glass pieces back in the bazaar in Harran when he'd been young, mostly overpriced little beads from Ur. His mom had a necklace of them.

But an actual bottle was… "Where did you get that?" His voice lowered to a furtive whisper.

An elfin grin tugged at Myrrha's cheeks, "Samas got them." She nodded to the chest where five other little bottles poked their thin necks out. "He met some traveling Egyptian healer years ago who told him how glass was *soooo* much better than clay pots, and he's been working on your dad to get them ever since. We managed to grab some off a desperate merchant from Byblos a couple years back. They keep plant oils fresh a lot longer."

Samas was the camp healer, a middle-aged man who lived in the next tent over and *claimed* to have studied under a master in Lagash. Personally, Joseph wasn't so sure. Samas must have been a pretty poor student to end up stuck living out here in tents with them. Unlike Myrrha and her mom, Samas wasn't a bond servant, so he could leave whenever he wanted. For some reason he hung around though, despite constantly protesting to the contrary, and he *did* seem to know his remedies.

"Still," Joseph shook his head, "they must have cost… what? Half their weight in silver?"

Myrrha grinned, "Like I said, he was a *desperate* merchant."

She glanced around to make sure no one else was watching, then unstopped the bottle, pulling out a plug of light tan wood from the stem with a faint pop that filled the tent with the concentrated scent of lavender. Her face scrunched with concentration as she trickled a few drops of yellowish oil into the crushed aloe before re-stoppering it and carefully putting it back. She shot him a conspiratorial glance. "Don't, uhh…mention that I was using that, would you?"

Joseph nodded and his friend quickly finished up her work, pounding the mixture into a sickly green paste.

Staring at it, Joseph wasn't sure what good that would be. "Are you sure you know what you're doing?"

Myrrha blushed, her cheeks tinging rosy red, "I think so. Samas has been showing me a lot of remedies." She bit at her lower lip a minute, like she was trying to remember something.

"Oh right," she exclaimed, turning and casting about until she found a little clay pot with a brown powder like sawdust inside. Grabbing a hefty pinch, she hastily stirred it into a cup of warm water and presented it to him, "I forgot, you're supposed to drink this first."

Yeah, definitely *not* encouraging.

Joseph eyed the clay cup with whatever the powder was floating in it. He shot her a skeptical look, but she seemed so excited at getting to do her own doctoring that he finally chanced a swig.

It was nasty, a bitter earthy taste. "Is this… wood?" he asked.

"Willow bark, actually," Myrrha said eagerly, "It helps with the pain." She nodded toward him. "Okay, let me see it."

Joseph dutifully lifted his tunic to reveal the thick bruise on his side. His mom would have gone into apoplectics if she'd been watching, but Myrrha kept a surprisingly cool head as she dabbed on the aloe paste.

It did hurt. He could tell she was trying, but Myrrha wasn't the most delicate touch. Joseph found himself wincing and gritting his teeth even after he quaffed down the rest of her painkiller drink. He wasn't sure if it was the willow bark or maybe just Myrrha being a bit more careful, but towards the end it did seem like the bruise hurt a bit less beneath the cool aloe gel.

By the time she finished wrapping his waist in the linen strip, his side was definitely feeling better. The sharp pain in his abdomen whenever he moved had faded to more of a background ache. At first even the constant pressure of the bandage had stung, but after a moment, it left him feeling better than before. He might almost be able to sleep through the night.

Myrrha tied off the cloth strip with a determined concentration and looked up. "How's that feel?"

In her enthusiasm she patted his side, and Joseph winced, "Oww."

"Sorry," she mumbled sheepishly. "How is it?"

"It's…" Joseph gave a tentative tap at his bandage, and certainly didn't feel as much pain as before, "it's not bad."

"Really?" she said, her cheeks dimpling with a grin.

"Yeah," Joseph said, more than a little impressed. "You did good."

Myrrha's smile widened until she was nearly beaming. For a moment, Joseph wanted to say more, but then her expression dimmed at something in the distance.

"Looks like the negotiations are over." Myrrha's voice dropped to a murmur.

Joseph followed her gaze towards his dad's tent. A tall, powerfully built man he recognized as Hamor, along with two of his lieutenants, was stepping outside, leaving Joseph's father, Jacob, standing at the tent entrance. They were far off but even so, Joseph could see that no one exchanged pleasantries as Hamor and his men mounted their horses and wheeled to leave. There were no angry parting words either though, so maybe they hadn't reached a decision either way. Reuben and Simeon were Dinah's oldest brothers and they'd probably expect a say in the whole thing too.

Joseph watched a moment as Hamor disappeared down the slope of the hill back toward Shechem. Then he looked back to Myrrha, whatever fragile moment they'd had shattered beneath the looming uncertainty of what came next. "I should probably go," he sighed. "I need to see my father."

She seemed to understand as he stood. "If you need to bathe, just sponge off and try not to get the bandages too wet."

He nodded, "I'll see you around, Myrrha."

For an instant the smile flickered back across her face, "You too, Joseph."

Chapter 4
A Price too High

It was dark, stuffy and miserably hot in the meeting tent when Joseph pushed aside the entrance flap and ducked inside. Fresh from a hasty sponge down, and wearing a clean change of clothes, the sweaty air struck him straight in the face as he entered. It was almost enough to make him leave, go back and talk with Myrrha or see his mom. At least there he could breathe. This was important though, too important to miss.

His father and the rest of his brothers had already arrived. Grim faced, they were arrayed in a loose circle on cushions which were normally a vibrant red in sunlight but were now stained blood scarlet in the gloom of the tent.

"Sorry I'm late," Joseph mumbled.

"Not at all." His father Jacob smiled and gestured him to sit. For anyone else, being last either meant having to squeeze in at the far end, the lowest spot in the group, or maybe upending someone smaller from their own seat. Today though, Dad patted the cushion directly to his right. His father had always saved it for him, ever since he'd been little.

Joseph strode across the tent and took his seat. He felt more than a few pair of envious eyes on him, but he figured it was fair enough. Little else went his way.

From the general dour expressions on the left side of the room, the discussion wasn't going smoothly, which explained why the front of the meeting tent had been closed off. It wouldn't do to let the servants see them arguing, even if that meant transforming the normally breezy tent into a melting sauna beneath the mid-afternoon sun. At least the temperature put a timer on how long they could stay cramped up in here. Might keep things from getting too heated.

"I assume you told Hamor to go drink goat *sinati* and expect company soon." Simeon, the second oldest, shot a dark glare across the meeting tent at his father."

From the way Joseph's dad arched his eyebrows, that apparently wasn't the best strategy to employ. "I most certainly did not," his father snapped back in a biting voice. "And if your plan is to start insulting guests under the protection of my tent, then you can leave right now, Simeon."

Simeon's expression went frost cold, even in the sweltering tent, and Joseph thought he might do just that. Leave and go do something stupid. A few breaths seemed to calm Simeon though, at least to the point where he pursed his lips and settled into more of an angry glower.

"I think," Reuben, the oldest, spoke up more measured, "what Simeon meant was, what's your opinion on all this, Father?"

Jacob exhaled, long and heavy. "My *opinion* doesn't matter," he said, slow and deliberate. "The reality is we are treading on very dangerous ground with Hamor, and we have more than just Dinah to consider."

"What is that supposed to mean?" Zebulun, the youngest of Dinah's brothers nearly spat from down at the far end of the circle. "We just leave her with that pig?"

"You have a better plan?" His father didn't rise to the bait and instead gestured with an open hand, offering him the floor.

Zebulun hesitated, caught off guard like he hadn't expected he'd have a chance to talk at all. Normally he probably wouldn't have spoken up, but Joseph knew he and his little sister were close. "I... I think we should go after her."

"I second that." Simeon raised a palm in fierce agreement. "I don't care whose firstborn he is. I won't stand by while that son of a goat rapes our sister." He shot a pointed look at Dad. "Unlike *some people.*"

The muggy tent went ice cold and Joseph could swear a chill scuttled down his spine.

For once his dad's calm mask cracked, his voice drew tight and dangerous, and Joseph saw his fists clench just a hair. "Would you care to elaborate on that, Simeon?"

Simeon was either too stupid or too angry to notice. "What I mean," he sneered, "is if it was... someone else they'd kidnapped," here he shot a pointed glare Joseph's direction, "then this wouldn't even be a discussion. But since it's *our* sister, all of a sudden you're talking in weasel words about–"

Joseph had never seen his dad move so fast, even with his limp. In a heartbeat Jacob went from sitting with a dark scowl to standing over Simeon, with fury in his eyes and the young man's tunic caught hard in his fist.

"Say that again," Jacob hissed.

Stunned silence.

When Jacob finally spoke, there was anger hovering right beneath the surface. Breathing heavily, he released Simeon and glanced around the room. "I do not want to hear any more *snide* insinuations that I do not care about MY OWN DAUGHTER!" His voice rose to a shout at the end. "Is that understood?"

No one answered.

Jacob slowly paced back to his spot and took a seat. "And I will hear no more talk of fighting either."

For a long moment no one spoke at all. Finally, the third oldest, Levi, who was sitting next to Simeon, raised a palm. "Father," he said, far more deferential, "with all due respect... why not? If you took up your bow, we would all follow you to a man. She's our sister, and you know this isn't right."

There was a low murmur of agreement around the room at Levi's words. That was the heart of it really. Dinah was a freeborn girl, and Hamor's son thinking he could just kidnap her and make her little more than his slave? That wasn't okay. And if they did nothing… what did that say?

Next to him, Joseph' father gave a long sigh, suddenly seeming far older than he had just an instant before. "I know," Jacob nodded. "And I wish that it was that simple. But I'm not going to lose any of you boys in a fight that we *cannot* win."

"Father," Levi insisted, "if we just kill Shechem–"

"Then it's war all the same," Jacob said bluntly. "Having spoken with Hamor, I assure you, he will not shrug off the loss of his firstborn son."

"But you don't think we can win?" Levi asked.

"Son," Jacob shook his head, "the city has walls, Hamor has his own stable, he can put fifty armed men in the field and another ten on horseback. Men who are actually trained to fight. We can put together what, maybe thirty, most of them shepherds, herdsmen, and hunters."

"And each of us can lay out three of Hamor's men with slings and arrows before they come close," Simeon spoke up. "That evens the odds."

"They'll have shields though." Dan, the oldest of the boys who wasn't Leah's, spoke up from Joseph's side of the circle. "And you've seen Hamor's armor. What good is a sling against that?"

For a moment the whole room devolved into a mumble of voices as they all fell into arguing the various points of a fictional battle. Could they spook Hamor's horses with their camels? How quickly could Hamor's spearmen close? Could they even defend their own camp from his riders? Maybe they could siege the city and starve them out, but then how soon would Hamor's own allies arrive? It was all too many ifs.

Listening to three different conversations at once, Joseph started to see things the way his dad did. It wasn't good, they were outnumbered almost two to one. Hamor's men were better armed, better trained, and Hamor himself was a renowned warrior.

Joseph knew the armor Dan had talked about. Hamor had led a small Canaanite alliance and taken it off the leader of an Egyptian raiding party years back. It was a rare piece, a coat of gleaming bronze plates that could turn aside a spear thrust, along with greaves, vambraces, and a helm to match. Just owning that alone made Hamor the wealthiest man in the city. And Joseph couldn't imagine how you were supposed to fight against someone covered head to toe in metal.

Joseph leaned over to whisper in his father's ear. "What are we supposed to do then?"

His father put a hand on his shoulder. "We talk. Hamor doesn't want a fight any more than we do." Jacob waited a moment until it seemed the confused discussions were starting to tilt his direction before holding up a hand. "So," he raised his voice and quickly quiet fell throughout the tent, "does anyone still think we can win a direct fight?"

Simeon looked sullen, but even he didn't raise a hand to contest the point.

Dad nodded, "In that case, Hamor has expressed his willingness to make amends. I told him to return with his son this evening to discuss taking Dinah as Shechem's wife. They are under my invitation and there will be *no* violence, *no* insults, *no* gross stupidity while they are here. *Is that understood?*"

He waited until he got eleven nods in the affirmative before looking to the six boys on the left of the room. "Reuben, Simeon, Levi, Judah, Issachar, Zebulun, she's your sister, so I'll leave it to you six to discuss what you think a fair bride price is along with reparations."

None of them looked very happy at that, but Reuben, the oldest, nodded his assent.

And just like that the meeting unofficially adjourned. No one wanted to stay in the sauna of a tent longer than they had to. In short order, Joseph's brothers had scattered outside, clustering in little pockets to discuss what came next.

Joseph stayed behind. It wasn't like he had anywhere to be. He busied himself drawing open the front wall of the tent, feeling the first whisp of a cool breeze sweep away some of the miserably muggy inside air.

"How was it?" his dad asked. "In the field?"

Joseph turned to see his father still seated. Some of the dour grimness from earlier had vanished to reveal the affable dad who'd clapped him on the back with a proud grin before he'd left three weeks ago.

"It was okay." Joseph walked back over and took a seat on the padded cushion. "I think I prefer it here though."

His dad chuckled, "I recall being of a similar opinion when I was your age."

Honestly, that didn't sound much like his dad at all. The only reason he wasn't out with the animals these days was because of his bum leg. You didn't notice the limp much when he walked around camp, but Joseph had seen him wincing at the end of long days outside. "What changed?"

"I met your mother." His dad abruptly pushed himself upright with a grunt. "Come on, I've been stuck in here all day."

Jacob paused a second at the tent entrance, a wistful look on his face as his eyes scanned across the camp that sprawled out in a rough oval before him. Most of the animals were housed in wooden pens a short walk beyond the tents, but quite a few others placidly wandered the camp. Sheep, goats, and more than a few strutting geese seemed perfectly at home munching on tufts of grass or pecking at grasshoppers.

The two walked together for a few moments in silence, making their way through the camp, his dad giving nods in passing while Joseph hung a half step behind.

Soon they were past the ring of tents, treading through the carpet of green grass on the valley floor. They didn't have to go far before the grass gave way to a patchwork of sycamore and oak trees that grew thick on the rocky hillside of Mount Ebal.

There, a hundred paces from camp, stood a waist high pile of stones loosely fitted together to form a flat surface. Once white, they were now blackened with soot. His father's altar to the God of their family, The God of the One who Struggles, *El Elohe Israel.*

His dad came here sometimes to offer sacrifices, but this time he simply took a seat, cross legged before the altar, staring at it for what seemed an eternity. Joseph waited, uncertain nervousness building as he stood. "Should I fetch a lamb, Father?"

For a long moment his father didn't answer, didn't move, seemingly completing a string of thoughts that couldn't be hurried. Finally though, he spoke a single word, "Sit."

Joseph did, his focus drifting from the altar, to his father and back, as he tried to puzzle out what his dad was thinking. How to deal with Hamor? Whether to try and rescue Dinah?

The questions hung like a cloud around the both of them. For a long time, his father gave no hints, until Joseph heard a woman's voice behind, his dad turning at the sound. "Jacob, is everything okay?"

Joseph's mom walked up slowly behind them, half supporting an old, wizened woman, who Joseph knew from his earliest memories simply as *Dede,* and whom everyone else called Deborah. She wasn't *actually* his grandmother, in fact she wasn't related to him at all, but she was about the closest thing he had. She'd been his dad's nurse years before, so she knew all the embarrassing secrets about him. And when Joseph had been little, Dede had always told the best stories, scary ones, that he wasn't sure could end well, right up until they did.

Joseph stood to help his mom, and in a moment she and Dede had both taken seats next to his dad. No one spoke. Finally, his mother glanced over at his father, still watching the altar. "You're worried, Jacob?" she asked in a quiet voice.

"Yes," he answered in a hushed but blunt voice. Jacob took a deep breath, then exhaled long and slow. "Do you think it was a mistake?"

Rachel looked confused, "You mean letting Dinah go to the town? Jacob, that wasn't–"

"Not that." He shook his head. "I mean staying here. Do you think it was a mistake?"

"I…" For once Joseph saw his mom unsure what to say. Her face twisted in an uncertain frown. "Where else would we have gone? To your brother at Mount Seir?"

Jacob stared long at the altar, like he was there but his mind was a hundred miles away. When he did speak his voice was barely a whisper, "We could have finished the journey."

Joseph's mom shot him a glance like maybe he could explain what his dad was talking about. When he shrugged though, she laid a hand on his dad's arm, her fingers small and delicate on his corded muscles. "Jacob, I thought this *was* the end," she said. "I thought this was home? The land of your father?"

There was a pleading note in her voice, and Joseph's dad blinked, the faraway glaze fading from his eyes. "I…" he shook his head like waking from a dream and turned to see the sudden worry written across her face. "Of course," he nodded. "This is home."

Joseph's mom watched for a few heartbeats, like suddenly she wasn't so sure. But Jacob laid an arm around her shoulders and pulled her close. "This is home," he repeated, reassuring.

Joseph saw his mom relax some, one hand holding her baby bump. She let out a deep sigh, and for a long time no one said anything.

Strangely, Joseph didn't mind. It was a rare thing to be alone with both his parents, and for a moment, all the infighting and struggles with his brothers were forgotten. They almost felt like a family. Almost.

Chapter 5
Soldiers of the City

Shechem and his father Hamor came, but not alone.

It was late afternoon when a squadron of ten men on horseback trotted out of the Low Gate and proceeded down the valley from Shechem towards their camp in a tight pack. They were followed by another twenty spearmen, carrying shields and clad in brown leather jerkins, painted with red highlights.

Watching from the edge of the forest along the low slope of Mount Ebal, Joseph flicked away the pebble he'd been fidgeting with and stood, squinting at a distant golden gleam among the mounted figures.

They'd gone out after Myrrha had finished her chores, to their usual spot on the mountainside, where a patch of low bushes made it easy to see but not be seen. With his brothers in a uniformly foul mood, Joseph had figured it was better to make himself scarce for a while. He'd long since learned all the best places for that.

Leaned up against a tree a few feet away, humming as she idly drew a thread out of a distaff matted with wool, Myrrha glanced up. Her face darkened and she swallowed audibly when she saw. "I thought just Hamor and Shechem were coming?"

Joseph tried not to look too nervous, even as he pushed down the lump of worry gathering in his stomach. "Probably just Hamor making a point," he said, even as he did a quick mental projection of how a fight might play out if Hamor meant to force the issue.

Probably somewhere between a bloody draw and a loss… for them.

Myrrha watched the small force moving like a snake down the road towards their camp. "Yeah," she said, unconvinced, "he sure brought along a lot of points to make."

As she spoke her finger spinning out the thin thread of yarn slipped, breaking the strand, and Myrrha let out a irate mumble, "*Tuhhu gizzatu*." Trashy wool.

"You know, I worked really hard to get that wool," Joseph said with a hint of good-natured indignation.

"Well, next time work harder on keeping the sheep from taking baths in a bramble thicket," she shot right back. "You know how many thorns I had to pick out of this?"

Joseph rolled his eyes. With Myrrha, one little prickle in her wool was too many. He looked back towards Hamor for a few heartbeats, his voice turning serious. "We should go."

Myrrha nodded wordlessly and stood, gathering her spinning distaff and a half spindle of fresh yarn, while Joseph waited a moment to walk her back. With a miniature army coming, it probably wasn't safe out here alone… or maybe it wasn't safe in camp, he mused grimly. Hard to say just yet.

It wasn't far back, and they paused near the outer ring of tents, Myrrha staring at him a long moment.

"Joseph," she finally said, "just don't…" Her voice died in her throat and her face twisted in a sort of uncertain frown, like she couldn't fit the words together quite right.

She could have meant a lot of things, but he knew her well enough to understand what she was trying to say, 'Don't get us all killed'.

That was a tall order actually. He felt like a solid half of his family were the sort to do exactly that, but he put on a confidence he didn't feel and nodded. "It'll be okay."

Myrrha bit her lip, unconvinced, but finally she nodded, turning back towards her own tent. And just like that, the two went their different ways.

The camp itself was more of a chaotic mess than usual, a muddle of nervous faces as Joseph made for his father's tent. No one was running to gather the bows and dole out arrows, though. Hamor's group wasn't far now, and stopping a moment to watch, Joseph was almost certain he could pick out Hamor and his oldest son Shechem, both at the front of the riders. It took a moment to register, but for some reason Hamor wasn't the one wearing his armor. Instead, that was a hulking, coppery clad figure on the horse behind him.

"Joseph!" An irate but familiar voice cut into his thoughts, and he turned to see Reuben, the oldest of them all, waving him over.

"Where have you *been*?" Reuben fixed him with a severe look. "Father's going out to meet Hamor and everyone needs to be there."

Before Joseph could come up with an actual answer, Reuben snapped a finger for him to keep up and stalked off.

A minute later Joseph watched from the eastern edge of camp as the column of riders and spearmen halted two dozen paces away. All but two.

Hamor and Shechem, a straight-backed, dark haired boy a couple years older than Joseph, clomped forward on their horses. Up close the horses were tall, imposing creatures with all the grace and beauty that a camel could never muster. Hamor reined to a halt a bare five paces from where Joseph's father stood, his walking stick in hand, though he wasn't leaning on it.

"Hamor," his dad's voice came out deadpan, unconcerned.

The older man on horseback met his greeting with a nod. "*Šulmu,* Jacob." He offered a greeting, his expression as unreadable as dad's.

Jacob gave a faint nod towards Hamor's… honor guard… muscle squad, Joseph was still making up his mind about the right description.

"I'm not sure we prepared food for quite so many," Jacob said, strangely calm.

Of all the things Hamor might have been waiting for, apparently that was it, because he gave a little flick of his hand and the rest of his horsemen and soldiers abruptly turned, heading back towards the city.

Hamor slipped off his horse, with a friendliness that almost seemed sincere, and shook his father's hand. "Well, I certainly wouldn't want to impose." Hamor said, his tone suddenly turning amiable, like they were best of friends.

It was an abrupt transformation. But behind Hamor's sudden warmth and Shechem's smug attempts at politeness, Joseph could read between the lines. Hamor might be here so his son could apologize, but he was still in charge.

Point made.

"What we want is our sister back!" Simeon demanded hotly, almost standing with pent up anger, his eyes fixed across the tent, on Shechem.

Sitting next to Hamor, Jacob actually *did* rise to his feet. "Simeon, sit down," he snapped, in a harsh tone. His eyes bored into his second oldest until Simeon's fists unclenched, barely, and he settled back, cross legged on his cushion. Even so, his forehead remained creased with a dark glower. Apparently, the wine wasn't doing much to soothe everyone's tempers.

An hour before, they'd walked into the meeting tent for the requisite welcome meal, and Joseph had been fuming when dad had seated him beside Shechem and Hamor. Easily his two *least* favorite people, even in front of Simeon and Judah.

But catching the bitterness in Simeon's voice, Joseph started to appreciate his father's foresight. There was a cold fire in his brother's eyes, an intense, unblinking rage that Joseph had learned long ago meant run, don't stop, don't look back – just run.

It was a look like Simeon dearly wanted to strangle Shechem. And if he hadn't been on the far side of the room, Joseph sensed he very well might have tried, consequences be damned.

The possibility was almost enough to make him snicker. Maybe that was his contribution to the negotiations– sit here and *don't* murder the guests.

Shechem seemed oblivious to how close he'd come to blows with Simeon. His father wasn't. Hamor hadn't spoken much during their elaborate dinner, no one had really, it made for an awkward meal. But now Hamor slowly stood to speak, his voice grave. "I understand this isn't what any of you wanted," he said, his eyes roving across the seated circle of Joseph's brothers. "And I know that the passion of youth is a poor excuse for my son's rash actions. But I ask you to set aside your grief for a moment," at this he glanced at Jacob. "My son Shechem has his heart set on your daughter."

"His way of showing it was foolish," Hamor cast a sharp glare down at his son, "and stupid. But he does love Dinah, and perhaps we can make something sweet of all this bitterness."

At the actual use of Dinah's name, Joseph saw his brothers, the whole far half of the tent, tense. Simeon in particular was coiled up like a viper before it struck.

Hamor just stared down their collective fury, outnumbered, but undaunted, his voice unwavering. In that moment, despite his distaste, Joseph started to understand why the men of the town would follow him.

"Please," Hamor spread his hands, "give her to him as his wife. Intermarry with us; give us your daughters and take our daughters for yourselves. You can settle among us; the land is open to you. Live in it, trade in it, and acquire property in it. Make a home here with us.

What is ours can be yours too, and together we can be friends and allies."

For a long second Hamor's words hung in the air, and Joseph blinked, not sure he'd heard right. After Hamor's show of force earlier, Joseph had expected more bluster and veiled threats. Certainly not… this.

For a moment Hamor's gaze roved around the tent, his eyes challenging each of them in turn. Joseph drummed his fingers, meeting Hamor's gaze as he considered the offer. It was a good offer.

He didn't feel right abandoning Dinah, but in truth he didn't see a way to get her back. Hamor could have brought her along if he'd meant to have a real negotiation. Instead he'd arrived with a squad of lancers. And now, here he was offering them the chance to… to have somewhere to call home.

Myrrha wasn't the only one to notice the men of the city looking at her differently. Joseph had felt their eyes also when he went into the town, the eyes of men who didn't trust them. Even with his dad around, he'd heard the whispers. The people in the market called them thieves. Farmers said their flocks ate the fields bare. More than once snide men from the city had shown up demanding a 'stolen calf' returned. And he'd heard more than his share of truly vulgar jokes about his family. He'd seen Hamor and his mounted guards arrogantly ride through the camp, uninvited, just to prove they could, and Dinah was hardly the first girl whom they'd given trouble, just the most important. Through it all he'd watched his dad counsel caution, even when Reuben and Simeon had pushed for revenge over all the petty sleights and small cruelties they'd endured.

They'd lived near Shechem for nearly ten years, almost as long as he could remember. It was more of a home than Harran, his grandfather's home, had ever been. Yet, in all that time, Joseph never really felt welcome.

And suddenly here was Hamor, finally holding out that olive branch, the one that meant they didn't have to live in goatskin tents forever. The one that meant people might give them fair prices at the market. The one that meant they could buy land and build homes behind the city wall, where it was safe. The one that meant people wouldn't look at them like they were savages.

Hamor speaking for them would mean a *lot*. It was sickening that it took their sister getting raped to make it happen but… Joseph pursed his lips, it was still a good deal, and looking around the tent Joseph could see he wasn't the only one to think it. Suddenly he was *very* glad Dinah wasn't his full-sister, and it wasn't his choice to make.

Next to Joseph, his half-brothers Dan and Naphtali spoke in muted whispers, from which he caught the hushed phrase, 'set up a shop in the city.' Meanwhile, across the tent, Reuben's face had gone from clearly angry to hesitant.

"And what of our sister?" Reuben asked, his eyes honing on Shechem. "She isn't a lump of silver to be bought and sold. And none of us will have her treated like a common–"

"Do you not understand?" Shechem suddenly spoke up in a loud, almost angrily sincere voice. "I love her!"

The whole meal sitting next to Joseph, Shechem had only uttered a handful of words. Mostly he'd managed to mistake Joseph for his half-brother Issachar, then rudely turned down a bowl of ewe's butter mixed with a tree spice that Dhra fondly called *daalacheenee,* but the traders simply referred to as cinnamon. Joseph still thought he was an idiot passing on that.

Through it all Shechem had looked smug, as always, but also… cagey, on edge, like a man sitting down to dinner with a pride of lions. Now though, for maybe the first time since he'd arrived that smugness was gone, replaced with a genuine passion. "Your sister means the world to me," Shechem said. "In my house she will want for nothing, she will have servants, honor, fine clothes. Her children – *your* nephews – will be lords of the city. Your nieces will marry the kings of Dothan, Luz and Jebus. I would love her and take her under my wing as my bride. Do me this favor, and I will give you whatever you want. Tell me what presents you want, and set the payment for the bride as high as you wish; I will give you whatever you ask, if you will only let me marry her."

Across the room, Reuben drew in a deep gulp of air, like he'd only just remembered to breathe, even while his fingers drummed absently on his thigh. Joseph could see the indecision in his eyes. It was an excellent deal, and it came at a terrible price. Legitimize what Shechem had done to their sister, give him their blessing, and marry into his family, or… fight… die? Joseph didn't see an alternative that ended well for any of them.

With the same questions hanging over them all, Reuben finally stood, his voice grave. "My brothers and I need a moment to consider this."

Hamor nodded his assent, and just like that, all six of Dinah's full brothers filed out. His father excused himself to follow them, leaving just Joseph, and his other four brothers to wait and make petty conversation with their guests about the weather and crops and grass. He felt strange, discussing trivialities, while not fifty feet away his family chose his fate for him. He told himself he'd done what he could in his own small way. Even so, the uncertainty hung over him like a sword dangling from a string – would his brothers return bearing peace… or war?

Chapter 6
The Lost Girl

Shechem awoke the following morning to find his bed cold. Blinking back his headache from the prior night's wine, he rolled over and reached across, expecting to feel the familiar warm lump that was Dinah. Nothing.

It took a moment to squint his eyes open against the morning glare spilling through the east window, but when he did, Shechem found his bed was empty, and a feeling like he'd swallowed a rock settled heavy in his gut.

Dinah was gone.

Instantly Shechem's eyes jumped from the patch of disturbed blankets, to the open east window, where the curtains were pulled wide, fluttering in the cool morning breeze.

Shechem tried to fight back a surge of dread that loomed cold as winter. She wasn't gone, he told himself. She couldn't be. The guards knew not to let her go. Even so, in only a few steps, he was out of his bed and at the window. Ignoring the majestic morning view of the valley, he peered out down the three story drop from the tower window to the packed earth street below. For a long moment he stood there in just his loose night tunic, staring, before finally shaking his head.

No. It was a ten pace drop to the ground and Shechem knew from personal experience when he was ten that she couldn't have climbed down the smooth white plastered walls of the tower. He tried to stay calm as he hurriedly dressed and descended the stairs to the second floor, where his father's day-cloak was already gone from its peg on the wall. Standing by the door, his mother, a tall, slender, dark haired woman with a severe, business-like air about her that never quite seemed to go away, was donning her shawl to leave with one of the younger slave girls at her side, basket in hand.

Shechem glanced around and swallowed. He still didn't see Dinah. "Where is she?" he asked, a hint of worry slipping into his voice.

His mother cracked an amused grin, knowing exactly who he meant without elaboration. "Downstairs." She nodded him in the right direction with barely a pause. It was quite a change from the first day when he'd brought Dinah home. Then his mother had been truly furious, his father too, but anymore she seemed more exasperated with his bride-to-be than anything else.

Hurrying down to the lower level of their palatial home, he ignored the lavish entryway and stepped into the normally steamy hot side chamber that acted as a kitchen. Except in the morning. Now the fires were cold, with only a few servant girls sitting in a tight cluster on the floor, grinding out flour for the day ahead. Over in the far corner though, he saw Dinah, still in her white nightgown. She sat huddled on the floor, frantically scrubbing at a copper pot with a handful of creek sand.

For a second Shechem stared, more confused than anything else. Finally though, his eyes returned to the slave girls who had suddenly gone dead silent. His expression hardened, and he stalked over to them, angry. "Is this your idea of a joke, Lasia?" he demanded, grabbing the oldest of them, a stocky young woman with northerner pale skin and brown hair. He wrenched her upright, a few inches from his face, finding fear in her eyes. "If I find you've been treating my wife like a common slave, it won't matter if Mother likes you, I'll have you–"

"No," The girl frantically shook her head and tried to pull away. "Please, it's not that."

"Then what is it?" Shechem demanded, his fingers tightening around her arm until tears welled in her eyes from the pain.

"Please," Lasia begged, half sobbing. "I tried to stop her, but she wouldn't listen, and I didn't know what to do and–"

Shechem didn't hear the rest. He loosened his hand in disgust and turned away, leaving a shivering Lasia to massage her arm as he marched over to Dinah.

The girl barely seemed to notice him as she scrubbed at her pot with a mix of sand and bubbly white lye.

"Dinah?" Shechem laid a hand on her shoulder and the girl finally seemed to notice him, shying away like a startled doe. Shechem felt a spark of anger at the glimmer of fear on her face when she looked at him. It wasn't supposed to be like this. "Dinah, what is this? What are you doing?"

"I…" Her voice trailed off after the single word like she wasn't sure herself. At her feet the copper pot was gleaming clean, but her hands were raw from the coarse sand and red from the harsh soap.

It was almost like she was in a daze. Shechem led her over to a clean water basin where he gently washed her hands of the burnt grime and grainy sand. "Dinah, you don't have to scour pans," he tried to explain softly, helping her back upstairs. "Lasia likes to pretend she's in charge, but if she tries to bully you, I'll have her scrubbing till her hands bleed." They walked back in to Shechem's room, not as opulent as his father's, but he still had plenty of years to fix that. Besides, with Dinah in it, the whole room seemed to almost glow like the sun, and in that instant Shechem wouldn't have traded being here with her for all his father's *things*.

"I know your brothers might have made you work back home," he stroked at her long dark locks, "but here, you're a princess."

Dinah gave a weak nod. But her eyes seemed drawn to the east window that looked out across the city, past the thick white stone and mortar walls, and off to her father's camp in the distance. Her gaze lingered there an instant longer than Shechem could stomach. Stalking over to the window, he pulled the linen curtains tightly shut, not that it did much good with the breeze. It left the room feeling darker though. He hated seeing her like this, it twisted at his gut, the feeling like it was all wrong and the wildflower of a girl he'd fallen for had withered and gone.

No, he resolved, not gone, still there. This was all just so much change so quickly. It was normal, he insisted to himself. She just needed some time, and then he'd find the old Dinah again. "I have some good news." He smiled and his words stirred an ember to life in those deep brown eyes.

"You do?"

Shechem nodded, "Yes, I have to leave for a little while today, but if things go right, we won't have to be separated again."

Dinah's face paled at the words, and Shechem tried to ignore the way her every muscle tensed when he pulled her close. He gave her a small kiss on the forehead anyway. "I know it's been hard," he whispered, "but things will be better." He paused a second, not sure what to say before settling on, "I love you." To which Dinah just gave a forlorn nod.

Still unsure what else he could do, Shechem left. Outside he could hear a rise in the volume from the street. That would be his father arranging a council, and he knew he needed to be there. He wasn't entirely sure how they'd sell the bargain they'd been offered the night before to secure Dinah's hand in marriage. Frankly, it was an extremely weird sort of deal. He assumed his dad would have a plan though, and no matter what, he *would* make things better with Dinah.

At the front door he was surprised to almost bump into a young woman about Dinah's age. She had shorter dark hair and wore a modest tan work dress that hung almost to her ankles. "Amaleigh?"

"Shechem." Her voice was cold but Amaleigh still offered a respectful curtsy.

He stared at her a heartbeat. As far as importance went, Amaleigh had very little business being *at*, let alone *in,* his house. Her father and older brothers were a part of their clan, and they farmed a few plots outside the city, which put him as a freeman with whom they were distantly related, but little more. "What do you want?"

Amaleigh frowned but nodded towards the door. "I'm here to see my friend."

Shechem hesitated, distrustful. That said, maybe a friend would help cheer Dinah up, help her find some familiarity in her strange new life. It might be exactly what his wife-to-be needed. Everyone knew it boded ill to have a gloomy bride. "Alright," he nodded, lowering his voice in case Dinah was listening at the window above. "She's been having a tough few days."

From the *you don't say* sneer that flitted across Amaleigh's face, he might also have added that the sky was blue and birds could fly. She hid it quickly, though. Shechem filed it away for later, but let it slide for now. "Maybe you can talk to her, help her adjust."

"Of course." Amaleigh offered another deferential curtsy.

Shechem nearly rolled his eyes at her sudden obeisance, anything to get in the door, he mused. She made to walk past him, but he grabbed her arm as she brushed by, his gaze locking on hers. "And Amaleigh," he whispered, his tone growing dangerous, "if I hear you've been poisoning her with any of your, *ideas* about men, you won't be back." A thin smile slid onto his lips, "And I'd hate to see your family have to pay the merchant price for grain next time the crops fail."

That was enough to put a hint of fear on Amaleigh's face as he walked away.

Good.

"They want us to do *what*?" a loud, indignant young man called from the back of the crowd. Several more voices mumbled their agreement.

Hamor raised an open palm to try and quiet everyone as he finished laying out the basics of the deal Jacob and his sons had offered them the night before. Standing next to him on a raised slab of white mountain-rock, Shechem looked out over the crowd gathered at the city gate and tried not to grimace.

"These men are our friends," his father insisted.

"Are they?" someone scoffed, a distinctive, rough, throaty voice from the back. Shechem didn't even have to search for the source. His eyes shot straight to Melqhath, a pudgy butcher, who had two nubs on his left hand where fingers ought to have been. He'd never heard precisely why, but his father clearly loathed the man, and the hatred seemed to be mutual.

There were perhaps thirty men assembled in all near the hulking mortared stone fortifications that surrounded the city. Although, of them, only about a dozen were of true importance, older men like his father and Melqhath whose words carried weight. The others were mostly young men, many of whom had young families of their own, but weren't truly elders. And of course, an impromptu cluster of his own rowdy friends at the back, mostly there for moral support and to offer the occasional whoop of agreement. Although… even they'd gone quiet when his dad had mentioned that the deal involved them all being circumcised.

That part had flown about as well as a rock, a particularly *dense* rock.

"They're cheats," Melqhath grimaced. "Everyone knows it, and I'm not about to submit to something like that just to get your son out of the cookpot he's jumped into."

Shechem felt a stab of anger at the words and stepped forward to speak. "If you think I'm just going to stand here while you insult my wife's family then–"

"Shechem." His father raised a hand for him to stop, and Shechem reluctantly drew his lips tight. Hamor's gaze slid back to the smug-faced butcher, and when his father did speak, his voice was strikingly calm. "And what would your plan be, Melqhath? Do nothing? Wait until they get angry enough to start sniping us off the walls, and we live under siege?"

Towards the back Shechem saw several farmers, among them Amaleigh's father, looking nervous at the prospect of a siege. Even if the city stood, they would see their fields burned… lose everything.

Melqhath didn't look too worried. "If you believe that's what it will come to, then let's ride out with lances and be rid of them."

Shechem nearly rolled his eyes. That was rich coming from the overweight butcher with a bad left hand, who hadn't so much as held a spear in years. And he apparently wasn't the only one who thought so.

"And what if Jacob's boys survive and hide in the forests up in the hills?" Amaleigh's father spoke up from the back. "I won't have my sons killed in the fields when they come looking for revenge."

Several more voices chimed in, "If any escape we could be fighting them for years. What happens when Esau in Seir hears we killed his brother and nephews? When the Egyptian raiders come back, they could guide them straight here."

Hamor shouted over the jumble of voices. "Everyone," he calmed them down and shot a pointed glare at Melqhath, "you all know me. You know I've never quailed before a fight, but we don't need to fight this day. These men are our friends."

"Let's invite them to live here among us and trade freely. Look, the land is large enough to hold them. We can take their daughters as wives and let them marry ours. But they will consider staying here and becoming one people with us only if all of our men are circumcised, just as they are. But if we do this, all their livestock and possessions will eventually be ours. Come, let's agree to their terms and let them settle here among us."

Shechem looked around the assembly as his father's words sunk in. Those were good points. He only remembered snippets from before Jacob's clan had settle near the walls of their city, but he knew well enough that trading with them had made their town prosperous. The market in the city square had grown, even in his own memory. And of course, there was the real opportunity staring them all in the face.

Jacob had eleven sons.

All of them would need wives in only a few short years, and someone as wealthy as Jacob could afford bride prices to make those of them with daughters *very* rich. His sons would inherit everything, come to live in the city, pay taxes, and in a generation they would all be one prosperous happy family, even despite their rough start.

It wasn't decided, but Shechem felt a flicker of anticipation that he and Dinah could be together after all, for real.

His foot nervously tapped at the rock, and despite it being morning, Shechem felt like the beating heat of the day was starting early. Finally, his father seemed to judge that enough time had passed and spoke up to call a decision.

"So, you have all heard the opportunity that is set before us. All in favor of welcoming Jacob as one of us?"

Only the elders were allowed to speak in the decision, but even so, a chorus of assent echoed around the courtyard by the gateway. Not unanimous, but close, and Shechem couldn't stop a grin from slipping onto his face.

"All opposed?"

No one spoke. Melqhath glowered, but apparently even he could see the direction the winds were gusting and wouldn't want to speak up for a side that had already lost.

"Very well." His father nodded, pleased. "So say we all?"

"So say we all," the elders intoned back.

Shechem breathed a sigh of relief at the words, and a triumphant feeling washed over him like a millstone had just been lifted off his back. It was done. Dinah was his.

Chapter 7
The Brothers Grim

Ignoring the uncomfortable pinch of the leather armor against his stomach, Levi crouched, half hidden behind the broad trunk of an oak tree. He stared out from the edge of the forest. Below, the northern slope of Mount Gerizim jutted out into the valley, running close to the walled city and offering a peerless morning view of the squat, white plastered houses and shadowed streets.

From three hundred paces it looked almost beautiful as the first rays of morning sun struck the valley. The off-white stone wall gleamed like a ring of pearl, and the house roofs were illuminated to reveal a blaze of colors. Dull red awnings stood shading Egyptian blue rugs and northern style, yellow-orange patterned robes, all hung out to dry where they wouldn't bleach in the sun.

Looming like a giant over the tightly packed houses rose the tower. A full four stories tall, it stood sentinel, keeping vigil over the valley. As Levi watched, his eyes marked out a flicker of motion at a third-floor window. A dusty yellow curtain was pulled aside and his breath caught in his throat…

His sister.

Around him the leaves rustled in the treetops. He watched from a distance as Dinah pulled her arms close against the crisp morning breeze. For a moment she didn't move, just stared out the high window towards their camp to the east. But only for a moment.

Something inside distracted her, and a moment later the curtains slid shut again. She was gone.

The scene was enough to spark a flash of anger in Levi's gut, seeing his baby sister trapped up in that tower with the boy who'd violated her. His grip tightened on the haft of the spear laid at his side. Father and Reuben might have been okay with bartering her away for money and peace; he wasn't.

Behind him Levi heard the soft tread of footsteps, and he glanced back to see Simeon approaching through the trees. Decked out with a razor tipped spear in one hand, two short swords strapped around his waist and wearing a boiled leather jerkin with molded arm and shin guards laced around his extremities, Levi's older brother cut a fearsome sight.

"See anything?" Simeon's voice was hushed as he knelt to watch the town.

"Third floor," Levi pointed. "She's in there."

Simeon nodded and laid a hand on his shoulder, his eyes sharp and focused, "We'll get her back. Did you see any of the men?"

Levi shook his head, *no*. Down below several of the women were already gathering near the town well to draw water for the day, indistinct snippets of their talking floating up the mountain slopes. Near the Merchant's Square, two younger girls scattered seed for the geese. None of the men were visible though, not even the farmers were out in the early morning. They all still looked to be laid up in bed after their mass circumcision three days before.

"Good," Simeon said, his tone grim.

Watching his brother glare daggers down at the quiet city, Levi started to understand his mother's last anxious words as she'd seen them off that morning, "Look out for your brother."

At the time he'd figured Simeon was about the last person who needed looking after. Now though, he caught a dark intensity on his brother's face, and understood. Simeon was coming back with Dinah, or not at all. There were no halfways.

Behind them came the loud crack of a branch beneath a heavy foot, and Levi winced at the noise as he looked back to see the rest of their party moving up behind them. Six others in all, four young burly herdsmen about his own age, as well as the tanner's apprentice, Joachim, and their chief huntsman, a tall, almost grey-haired man named Nashu, volunteers all.

Joachim had managed to secure them the leather breastplates and armguards they now wore. The hardened leather was ill-fitted, felt awkward to wear, and in Levi's own case, dug painfully into his gut whenever he crouched. It wasn't anything to match Hamor's vaunted coat of bronze plates for strength, but leather was one thing they had that was *never* in short supply, and it *would* stop a spearpoint. They'd tested it the prior day.

Moving almost to the tree line, the rest of their little squad lowered the short ladder they were carrying. It was crude, basically thick sticks lashed together with copious amounts of rope, but with the city gates locked and barred, it was their only way in. Shabby as it looked, Levi knew it could hold his weight and it was the best he'd been able to piece together the prior day as they tried to stealthily assemble their operation. Obviously, Father wouldn't have approved, so they'd had to improvise.

Nashu passed through the small group, bow slung across his back, quietly passing out bronze tipped spears from a bundle before moving up to join the two brothers. Of them all, he at least, seemed to move comfortably in the armor. He even wore a distinctive blue and white, beehive-shaped cap, an heirloom of his time in the Kaftorian High Fleet out of Knossos.

Nashu knelt next to them, fingering the needle-like bronze sword at his side as he took in the situation.

"Once we're inside the wall, they'll come at us from every direction," he said in a professional tone.

"They'll be too hurt to come at us at all," Simeon said dismissively.

Nashu cocked an eyebrow, skeptical, but before his brother could say more, Levi stepped in to be the voice of reason. He found himself doing that a lot lately. "Why don't you take three others and act as the rearguard. We'll stay tight in the streets and make for the tower. Simeon and I will deal with Shechem and Hamor inside, while you clear out the rest of the city."

"You don't want help?"

Levi took one glance at the barely veiled fury in his older brother's eyes. "We'll be fine."

Nashu nodded and slipped back to organize the ladder carriers. As he did, Simeon finally drew his flinty glare away from the compact, walled city. "You'll need this, Levi." He unbuckled one of his bronze swords and handed it over.

Levi managed a blustering grin as he hefted his spear. "I think I'd prefer something with a bit more reach."

Simeon insisted though. "Take it. For when we get inside."

Levi hesitated a second, before shrugging and buckling on the blade in its leather scabbard.

When he finished, Simeon looked him over with approval before gesturing to the spear at Levi's side. "Don't forget to drop that when the time comes."

Levi wasn't sure why dropping his spear would ever be a good idea, but nodded anyway. An anxious apprehension started to sink in. They were doing this. For real.

Simeon stood and gestured the ladder bearers up with a flick of his wrist. Nashu spent a few heartbeats silently getting their other five retainers in line, before giving an 'all set' acknowledgement with his pointer finger.

Taking a last deep breath and gripping his spear tight to stop his hand shaking, Levi felt his brother brush up next to him with a nudge. Simeon had his eyes fixed on the city with a wild, wolfish grin. "Come on, little brother," he whispered. "Let's get her back."

Simeon broke cover first with Levi close behind. His instinct was to sprint, but his brother kept a measured jog through the knee height grass scattered with loose stones. Behind them there were no shouts or battle-cries from Nashu and the ladder bearers, just the steady swish of grass and the pat of sandaled feet on the turf.

He kept expecting screams and shouts of panic from the city, but none came, just a few jumbled women's voices, muted by the light breeze.

Then they were there.

The city wall always felt taller up close. Ten feet of white mortared rock, two feet thick, while a low parapet at the top provided cover for the defenders. Behind them came the ladder. Joachim was puffing a little, but otherwise everyone looked fresh like they'd just rolled out of bed.

In just a few heartbeats and a flurry of gestured signals, Nashu had the ladder up. The top gently bumped against the wall barely a hand-breath below the parapet. Simeon scaled the wall in a flash, and before he quite had time to think it through, Levi was after him, pulling himself up onto the top, which was really just the roof of one of the many houses that were built into the wall to ring the town. Not really that different from the way their own camp was laid out, except spaced closer and done in heavy stone.

Behind them Nashu scrambled over, followed by the rest of their contingent. Taking the lead, Simeon made for the set of stone steps down into the city proper. Two paces behind, and moving soft as a lion on the prowl, Levi followed. He'd just put one foot on the packed earth street, when the door of the house to their left abruptly swung open. They all froze as a portly, middle aged woman emerged, a clay water jug in one hand.

In an instant her eyes caught them, her pupils going wide as bowls. Simeon rushed at her, bringing up his spear and the woman screamed, a terrified, high pitched wail. It only lasted for a blink before his spear-butt cracked her under the chin, and she dropped like a sack of grain.

But it was enough.

The shriek shredded through the morning calm like a pride of lions through a flock. For an instant, Levi's eyes locked on the figure of the limp woman. Until a hand shoved him from behind and Nashu's sharp voice sliced through his daze. "Move!"

Levi stumbled into the street, while Simeon started barking orders, his spear raised skyward like a banner. "Levi, Davor, Joachim, on me!"

"Stay close!" Nashu shouted, frantically trying to organize everyone as the rest of the party spilled down into the town. "Move together! Fight together!"

Above that Simeon's voice rang like a hammer on bronze. "To the tower!"

Simeon stalked ahead, heedless of anyone else. Levi followed close to cover his brother, as all around more shouts of confused panic echoed from the houses.

A few paces ahead a door burst open and a little girl in a tan tunic darted out shouting, "Mama, what's…"

Simeon's spear butt smashed her aside, knocking her to the ground. She shrieked in pain. Five steps behind a man chased out after her, "Ira get–"

His voice stopped dead at the girl curled and wailing in the dirt. Then he threw himself at Simeon like a madman.

From the way he walked it obviously pained him to even move, but with his daughter screaming in the street, that suddenly didn't matter. Before Simeon could get his spear back around, the man had both hands on

the wooden haft, fighting wildly to jerk it from his
brother's grasp.

"Get back!" Levi shouted, trying to ward off the
man with his spearpoint. He jabbed at him, just as the
man knocked Simeon off balance. The two staggered to
the side, and Levi felt a sharp tug on his spear as the
man slammed into the razor tip.

Levi's breath drew sharp, and for a single heartbeat
it was like the world slowed to a crawl. Simeon firmed
up his footing and shoved back, desperately struggling
for his weapon. For an instant the man barely seemed to
notice the bronze point jabbed in his side, even as the
blood poured out. But his grip must have weakened,
because Simeon wrenched his spear free and shoved the
man away. In a flash he lashed his spear-butt against
the man's head with a sickening *thunk*, and Levi's
spear-point was dragged to the ground as the man
collapsed, dying.

Simeon glanced around, like he was already nerving
for the next fight, but Levi's eyes were still fixed on the
motionless figure. Somewhere nearby he heard the little
girl's screams, an awful anguished noise to tear at his
heart.

He'd never killed someone before. A part of him felt
terribly wrong, but before he could really think, he
heard a deep enraged voice shout in the street ahead.
"LYING CURS!"

He looked up to see two other men struggling
towards them. Clearly the circumcision had left them in
pain, they winced at every step and waddled about like
they could barely walk.

But they were coming. Something deep inside Levi
hardened at the sight. They'd brought this on
themselves, he resolved. These were the men who'd
stood by while Shechem treated his sister like a whore.

He jerked his weapon free from the dead man at his
feet, and the world seemed to narrow to just the street
as both he and his brother lowered their honed

weapons. Levi felt the rush of nervous energy in his arms, his spear suddenly light and easy to wield as the men approached, fury written on both their faces.

But Levi felt a fury too. As the men hesitated just beyond spear reach, he let his fury drive him ahead.

Levi screamed and charged.

Chapter 8
The Men in the High Tower

It was stupid, his attack. Against a real warrior he would have died. But the men of the city weren't warriors, not today.

Somewhere in the dim back of his mind Levi recognized the man he faced, an older farmer, Panat. They'd always been on good terms... before. But suddenly they were on opposite ends of the spear.

Panat desperately thrust his spear to stop the charge, but Levi had been dueling his brothers with quarterstaffs since as long as he could remember. A spear wasn't much different, just sharper.

The stroke came almost by instinct, Levi struck hard, knocked the farmers spear aside and in the same motion twirled the wooden end up to smash him beneath the chin.

He ended the fight in little more than a blink, and as Panat dropped, brought his lance tip around to run him through where he lay.

Next to him, Simeon had easily dispatched his man and was already pressing on. Somewhere behind he heard the twang of a bowstring, followed by another man's screams of pain. The noise drowned behind the shouts of the herdsmen, as they took up a war-cry in an eerie unison, "JA-COB! JA-COB! JA-COB!"

The city wasn't very large, and they were already close to the wide open Merchant's Square.

Turning to wave the rest forward, Levi saw Nashu's little squad swarm another man of the city, unarmored and still in his bed-tunic. "Nashu!" he screamed over the din. "Rally to the square!"

The old Kaftorian hunter raised his bow in acknowledgement, then nocked an arrow, and that was the last Levi saw as he turned away. Simeon was already a score of paces ahead, with Davor close behind. A few feet away Joachim looked rooted in shock, and Levi rapped him across the arm with his spear-haft to snap him out of it. "Joachim! With me!"

Levi didn't wait to see if the tanner's apprentice was following. He sprinted to catch Simeon, passing a side street where he caught the two girls who'd been feeding geese fleeing in terror. In a few dozen more paces he caught Simeon, and the footpath opened up into the Merchants' Square.

While the city streets were barely wide enough to wheel a cart through, the merchants square was almost extravagantly massive. Set near the foot of Hamor's keep, Levi blinked when he saw it nearly deserted. He'd only ever been here on market days, when the whole town seemed to be gathered. Women would bustle by as they picked over the wares of traveling merchants, while men got into shouting matches, haggling over price.

Now though, it stood disconcertingly barren, the stalls mostly packed away. Near the center, a few nervous men had rallied at the mingled shouts of confused panic that rung across the city. "Attack!"

A dim part of Levi's mind counted seven men, looking more lost than ready, but still armed. Not the best odds.

Before he could even think it through, Simeon was already out in front, taking up the shouts of the others, "JA-COBBB!"

Simeon charged them all – alone.

Levi cursed and rushed after his brother.

If they'd stood as one, Simeon wouldn't have stood a chance, but Levi had seen Simeon like this before, fearless and furious. Alight with a rage that a dozen spears couldn't stop.

The men of the city scattered.

Levi threw himself into the fray and went after a boy about his own age. Massin, the name dimly flickered to mind, the brother of one of Dinah's friends.

Despite wincing when he walked, Massin faced him with a leveled spear and a speed bred of desperation. Levi struck, his spear sweeping out an arc towards the boy's face. Massin blocked with the sharp crack of wood on wood and thrust back. His spear punched at Levi's chest like a kick from a goat.

Levi barely felt it though. He twisted and rushed close, the point gouging his hardened leather breastplate as it slid off. Then he slammed his whole body into Massin, and the boy shouted as they crashed to the dirt. Writhing, Massin tried to bring his spear around, but they were too close to use the razor point. Levi dropped his own spear to the ground, whipped out his short sword and ended it with a sharp thrust.

He rolled to his feet, sword in hand, even as another man cracked a spear-pole painfully at his arm. Levi tried to back away, tripped over Massin's body and crashed hard on the packed ground. He rolled away as the man stabbed at him and found only dirt.

Even struggling to walk, the man still managed to run Levi down. Standing over him, the man smirked as he pulled back his spear to strike again. Then his mouth abruptly dropped open, his face twisting in a pained grimace as the spear slipped from his hands. He collapsed forward to reveal Joachim, pulling his own bloody weapon from the man's back, his face ghostly pale.

There was only time for a grateful nod as Levi grabbed at his own spear a few feet away and scrambled upright. Across the square, Simeon was basically an army unto himself. His spear twirled into a blur as he fought off two men at once, with another two bodies laid out on the ground. Ten paces away Davor was still standing, but clutching at his bloody upper arm with a motionless corpse at his feet.

When Levi looked around though, all he saw were more men of the city closing in from every direction. His small squad had all the advantages – armor, surprise, organization, and it was clear the circumcisions hadn't left anyone in the best shape to fight. But even so, in the grand scheme, they were outnumbered at least eight to one, maybe as much as twelve to one. He'd known that all along, but as more soldiers rushed into the square it started to sink in what those numbers actually meant. Already Levi was breathing hard, but there was nothing else for it. Simeon was off in a wild frenzy, which just left him to pull things together.

"Davor, Joachim! With me!" Levi fumbled a heartbeat to slide his blade back into the leather sheath, then twirled his spear. "Fight them as they come!" he frantically shouted above the din. "Charge!"

As the numbers swelled against them, Levi desperately threw himself against two others, a pair rallying to the square bearing quarterstaves. The two rushed at him and he desperately warded them off, running one through before being flanked and painfully knocked on his back. It might have ended there, except for Davor who rushed to his rescue, stabbing the second one down with a spear clutched in his one good arm.

When Levi did struggle back to his feet, things looked worse than ever. Simeon was still fighting like a lone madman, but across the square another eight or so men had grouped up, spears bristling out like barbs on a cactus. Already battered and badly bruised, Levi sucked in air as his tired fingers tightened around his spear. He knew what he had to do.

He leveled his spear-blade and glanced at Davor, wounded, and Joachim, terrified. "Charge together!" He tried to capture something of the authority he knew from his father's voice. "Fight together!"

Levi raised his spear to the attack with the defiant scream, "DI-NAH!"

Then the buzzing hiss of an arrow shaft cut the air. One of the men of the city screamed in pain, stumbling out of their impromptu formation. The rest of Nashu's squad, slammed into their flank in a storm of flashing spearpoints.

Crashing into the wild melee, Levi batted aside a spear-pole before dispatching the owner. Then he squared off against a giant of an older man who, despite missing a few fingers, still twirled a meat cleaver like he meant to carve them up.

The man swung at him, throwing his whole body into the strike as he taunted and swore. His face looked almost gleeful at the fight. "Come here you little pile of *zû*."

Levi dodged back, trying to get range for his spear, even as the man stumbled forwards. He jabbed and caught the man's arm, but the three fingered man just roared in pain and smashed ahead, heedless. The first strike of the cleaver neatly chopped Levi's spear in half. Then the zip of an arrow took the man in the chest, and Davor got in a finishing blow from behind.

Caught in a pincer, the men of the city scattered. For at least a moment, Levi could breathe. They held the square.

Before he could so much as stop panting, Nashu's sharp voice called. "Levi! The tower!" He turned to see the old hunter gesturing with an arrow towards the hulking stone building in front of them. "Before they can bar the door! We'll hold here!"

Almost before he finished speaking, Nashu's eyes honed in on something behind Levi. Deftly nocking one arrow, he sent it lancing upwards, and Levi spun to see an archer poised on a nearby rooftop stagger backwards, vanishing behind the low roof-wall, an arrow in his chest.

Snatching a discarded spear from the ground, Levi forced his legs forward to where Simeon had fought all comers and somehow emerged alive. There were five bodies scattered around, his leather armor scored deep in at least three spots. A nasty gash dripped blood from the back of his hand and another trickle of scarlet ran down his cheek from what looked like a staff blow straight to the forehead.

Simeon hardly seemed to notice, his whole expression caught up in the ecstasy of the fight. A grim glee that unnerved even Levi.

"We got them good, little brother." Simeon was breathing hard as Levi approached, and more shouts of fighting echoed in the square.

Levi just nodded and followed his brother's gaze as it narrowed on the Tower. A burning glare, like he'd tear it stone from stone with just his eyes. "Let's finish it."

The heavy wooden door wasn't locked. Probably one of the servant girls had opened it when she'd gone to fetch water. Shoving it open, the two boys stepped into the dim light of the corridor to find a short hallway leading to a flight of stone steps, with several other doors branching off to side rooms.

As they stepped inside, there was a frightened squeal, and Levi's eyes snapped to a half open door on the left in time to see a girl vanish back into the side room, a wisp of a tan work skirt and raven hair.

He nodded at the room and Simeon moved to cover him, wordless. Levi gripped his spear tight, moved close to the door, then nudged it open. The hinges groaned as it creaked wide to reveal a cluster of servant girls huddled in the far corner of the kitchen, staring back at him with glimmers of fear in their young eyes.

They didn't scream though, no shrieks of panic, just watching, wondering. Meeting their gaze for a long heartbeat, Levi raised a finger to his lips for quiet, then stepped back, and nodded Simeon towards the spiraling stairs that led upwards.

The shouts and screams outside sounded faint and faraway as they mounted the narrow steps. Simeon was in front as they rounded the landing to the second floor. They discovered an open space that would have served the same purpose as their meeting tent, a low table surrounded by cushions. Bright morning light streamed through the east window, illuminating the room. It was empty, not even servants to be found.

Levi's eyes rapidly scanned the room, then the two continued upwards. On the third floor, they found a circular central room, twenty feet wide with four side doors leading to smaller rooms. The doors were shut. All but one. Inside Levi caught a glimpse of the dark hair and olive skin he could never have forgotten.

"Dinah." He crossed the room in only a few paces, even as she spun towards him, horror written on her face, "Levi no! They–"

Her voice was lost as another door banged open, and Levi turned just in time to take a spear straight to the chest so hard that it knocked him back. He felt a sting like a needle through the rigid leather armor.

At the other end of the spear was Shechem, his face a mask of rage. Somewhere nearby more roars echoed in the room. Hamor's deep voice flung obscenities as he stormed down the stairs and set upon Simeon. "You worthless sons of *kalbati*!"

Levi tried to strike back, but Shechem was already bringing around his spear-butt for a finishing blow. Levi threw up his arm to take the bone-jarring strike on his armguard.

"You liars!" Shechem raved, shoving Levi back against the wall with a shocking strength, their spears too close to matter. "We gave you what you wanted."

Panicked, Levi slammed his knee at Shechem's groin, but his opponent was standing sideways and Levi only grazed him. Even so, he must have struck a tender spot, because Shechem's face twisted in pain, even as he smashed his spear haft against Levi's throat, "Cowards!" He shouted right in his face, as Levi felt his wearied arms start to give out, the spear crushing closer to choking him.

He heard Dinah's desperate scream, "Shechem NO! Please!"

Shechem hesitated.

For a half second the press of the spear weakened at Levi's throat, and in that instant he remembered. His sword.

Throwing every ounce of strength he had into it, Levi mustered a single shove back against the wooden pole at his neck and dropped to the floor. Shechem stumbled forward, even as Levi whipped out his blade and struck.

Shechem screamed and doubled over, even as Levi struck again. Somewhere by the stairs he heard an anguished woman's wails, a mix of pain and fury.

As Shechem died, Levi looked up to see a woman he dimly recognized as Hamor's wife sweeping across the room, vengeance in her eyes and a carving knife in her hand.

He raised his blade to force her back, but in her grief, she didn't seem to care. She threw herself at him, and his sword struck home, even as her knife slid off his breastplate and sliced at his arm. Levi stumbled away, a deep gash beneath his shoulder flowing blood, even as the woman sunk to the ground.

Across the room, Simeon and Hamor were still locked in a violent contest, Simeon's speed and youth barely hanging on against Hamor's weight and experience. Grabbing a spear from the ground, Levi forced himself to stand.

One last thing. Bring Simeon home alive.

He'd promised.

Chapter 9
Paradise Lost

Joseph swung the flax mat hard against the rough tree trunk, his face turned away so he wouldn't breathe in the cloud of dust that poofed out at each blow. For an off-white mat, there was a *lot* of dust.

Ten paces upwind, Myrrha was idly raking a comb through a wool fleece. The comb pulled off small white tufts that she delicately picked clean, before cross-hatching them into a layered woolen mat. Eventually she'd bundle it all up on her distaff to spin out yarn, but for the moment the fluffy wool made it look like she had a little cloud in her lap.

Swatting the mat against the oak tree a few more times, Joseph leaned against the trunk to catch his breath. He brushed off the fine layer of grime collecting on his tunic, just as Myrrha drew a sharp breath, scowling and mumbling about thorns as she flicked something away.

Joseph sighed and stooped to pick up another mat from his copious pile, when Myrrha finally spoke up. "Do you think your mother would go for something blue?"

"Huh?"

"Maybe for the baby? A little blanket or something?"

Joseph stared at her a heartbeat, eyebrows raised, skeptical. Myrrha was good at weaving, very good, but she moaned incessantly whenever she had to make things for someone else. "Since when are you so eager to be helpful?"

Myrrha frowned and rolled her eyes, "It's not–" A brisk morning gust abruptly caught up the miniature cloud of wool, and she hurriedly pressed it back into her lap. "Just," her cheeks tinged red, "I've been wanting to make this shawl. It'll be gorgeous. I'll do these blue and yellow swirls on the chest and… well, I've got the thread and the yellow dye, but I need some blue." She gave a resigned sigh, "I know your father won't get the dye if it's just for me. I figured if it was for the baby though, maybe I could get some extra and…"

Her voice trailed off, like maybe it wasn't such a good idea.

Joseph lifted the next mat from his copious stack. For a heartbeat he could swear he heard something like a shout, but it was lost on the wind.

"Mom would probably take a blanket," he said as he set to forcefully whacking it against the oak tree.

"You think?" Myrrha's voice brightened.

"Don't see why not." Joseph worked another few minutes, finally pausing as a particularly thick dust cloud settled around him. Stepping back and panting hard, he leaned over, elbows on his knees as he glanced her direction. "I don't suppose you were going to help at some point?"

Myrrha was suddenly very focused on her wool, a guilty look on her face like when he'd caught her trying to squirrel away a basket with half the camps' sewing supplies last year. She squirmed, "Not really."

Joseph let out an exasperated huff and gave the mat another stiff whack. It was still dusty, "Well, what good is that? I've got sixteen more of these."

Myrrha gave an unsympathetic shrug. "Maybe you shouldn't have said Asher was as stupid as an… an *ušāru*." Her cheeks blushed a furious scarlet at even saying the word aloud.

"Well, he is." Joseph let out some of his frustration with a few more whacks of the mat before laying it aside.

"That doesn't mean you had to say it," she insisted with a hint of sarcasm. "At least not in front of Leah and Zilpah. Joseph, you already know neither of them like you."

"Don't worry," he grumbled, leaning down to grab another mat. "I know."

Apparently Myrrha wasn't satisfied with his answer. "I'm not sure what you expected. I mean, you don't hear me going around insulting half the camp to their faces."

"Well, that's because you're a…"

Joseph caught himself before the rest slipped out. He'd meant it as a joke, but now a long pause hung between them.

"A what?" Myrrha asked, her voice suddenly frosty, "A slave?"

"Myrrha, I didn't mean–"

His voice died in his throat as he tried to figure out what *exactly* he hadn't meant.

He hated these moments. Sometimes it felt like they were just friends, trying to make their way through things together. Then this would come up, and suddenly they'd be standing mountains apart.

"I'm sorry," Joseph finally said.

"It's fine." Myrrha snapped in a voice that obviously wasn't. She focused back on her wool, and Joseph grabbed another mat.

He paused though, at a noise like a shout drifting from the city. It was almost lost to the wind, but this time Joseph was certain he'd heard it. Listening he caught more screams, and not the happy, harvest-feast sort.

"Myrrha do you hear…?"

He glanced back to see his friend suddenly sitting at rapt attention. The wool lay forgotten in her lap as her eyes fixed on the city. He didn't have to finish the question.

The two weren't more than fifty paces from the ring of tents that marked their camp, and Myrrha hastily bundled her wool into a reed basket as they stood to go.

They found the camp to be in equal confusion, some people groggily crawling out of their tents while Reuben stalked past with a spear in hand and Issachar close behind. "Go get something to fight with and get back here with Zebulun," Reuben snapped, as they hurried past.

He lost Myrrha in the confusion, and with the anguished screams from the town growing ever louder, Joseph headed for his mother's tent, not really sure where else to go.

He never made it.

"Joseph!" He turned just as his half-brother Dan tossed a spear his direction and Joseph fumbled to catch it midair.

"Dan what's going—"

"No idea." Dan cut him off, just as his younger brother Naphtali jogged up with a bow and quiver, ready for a fight. "You're with us though. We're going to the city."

That… didn't strike him as the best plan. But, as far as his convoluted family went, Dan and Naphtali were about as close to allies as he had. Dan had stuck up for him more than once, and if they wanted his help…

"What do we do?" Joseph gripped the spear haft and glanced toward the walled city barely a ten-minute walk up the valley.

"Stay close," Dan said in a terse voice, "and try not to die."

The front gate was barred when they arrived outside the walls. It had only been a short jog, but Joseph already felt like he might puke. A stab of nervous tension roiled his stomach. The screams were louder now, sharp women's wails that cut the morning air like a knife mingled with deeper men's voices. Familiar men's voices.

Naphtali hung back a dozen paces, an arrow nocked to his string. Dan lifted his spear and gave a loud bang on the heavy wooden gates, which quivered at the strike.

"Open up."

For a heartbeat, no one answered

Then he heard an earthy *thunk* from the opposite side. Joseph's fingers tightened around his spear as the gate inched open, and out stumbled Simeon and Levi escorting Dinah. Behind them spilled out an entire squadron of familiar faces in scarred leather armor.

They looked awful, bruised with cuts in a half dozen places, and soaked with sweat like they'd just sprinted up the mountainside.

Still, Simeon somehow managed a triumphant half-grin at seeing them. "Good." He was breathing heavily and bleeding from a nasty cut on his shoulder. "We could use some help."

Dan stared at them, disbelief written in his eyes. "What happened?" he finally managed.

Simeon gave a wolffish grin, "We have our sister back." He nodded towards Dinah, who was huddled next to Levi looking more numb than alive.

Simeon didn't seem to notice. He idly dug his spearpoint into the dirt and made a grandiose gesture back to the gate, where the screams and sobs still hung in the morning air. "We have our sister back, Shechem is dead, and the city is ours."

Chapter 10
Children of the Ashes

Joseph felt eerie, picking through someone else's stuff. Taking a little rag-doll from a cabinet he stared at it a moment. Just this morning, it had belonged to someone else, all of it– the doll, the cabinet, the house, the silver that Dan and Naphtali were tearing the back room apart to find.

There was probably some little girl who loved that doll, some carpenter who'd spent hours on the cabinet. Now the carpenter was dead, the little girl was a slave, and somehow he was supposed to decide what was trash and what was worth keeping. It all left him more than a little queasy.

"Joseph!" Naphtali's harsh voice snapped him out of his daze. He started, glancing over to see his half-brother staring at him with skeptical eyes. "Were you going to help, or just stand there all day?"

"I… sorry." Joseph hastily set the doll back on the cabinet and glanced around, searching for something useful to work on.

Naphtali just rolled his eyes and gave an exasperated sigh. "If you want the stupid doll, keep it." He turned away, "I suppose the baby might enjoy it. It's no good to anybody now."

Joseph hesitated a heartbeat, staring at the doll before finally taking it and dropping it into his sack. He… maybe the baby would like it, and he didn't feel right just leaving it to rot, not if it had mattered to someone. He rubbed at his forehead like it might dispel all his questions and set about tugging the cabinet away from the wall. They were looking for loose boards, a hidden crevice, anywhere that might hide whatever silver the people who'd lived here had.

It probably wasn't much, he mused. Might not even be worth the hassle they were going to. If these people had small children, he doubted they had a lot to hide.

Still, it was better than the alternative of rounding up everyone left. Joseph was grateful Reuben and Judah were doing that part.

Maybe it was just that he knew these people. Well, sort of. He didn't know that many of the girls, and all the boys he'd known were dead, so… it all felt really twisted.

He'd heard Reuben's whole explanation about how the women and children didn't have anywhere to go, so they'd be camp servants. But seeing the women sobbing and blank-faced with grief, Joseph didn't feel like they were doing them any great favor.

Pushing the cabinet back into place, Joseph didn't realize until the third shove that there was no real point. Nobody lived here, nobody cared. Not anymore.

Leaving the cabinet where it sat, he wandered into the next room. There were only three rooms in the house, and he could see his half-brothers through the open door, ransacking the place. They'd already been through here and left a trail of mess in their wake. If only their mother could see them now, Joseph mused, humorless.

His eyes roved across the wreckage. Then he spotted it, a woven basket, flipped upside down but with a bundle of thread peeking out beneath. Turning it upright, he found a treasure of knitting supplies, needles, days' worth of already spun out thread and a few delicate, half embroidered pieces. Beneath it all his hands found a collection of little clay pots with their lids still miraculously on.

Opening one, Joseph found red, then yellow and looking in the third he couldn't hide a smile at the Egyptian blue powder that greeted him. Dan and Naphtali had probably looked here, decided there was no money and trashed it.

Idiots.

The dyes were probably worth more than whatever silver scraps they found. It was also exactly what Myrrha had been asking for. Maybe it was a sign that he'd been spending too much time with her, but he could even pick out a bolt of fine cotton cloth in there. That was from the east, *really* far east. Beyond Akkad.

Grabbing the basket, Joseph decided he might as well take it before his half-brothers decided to burn the place down just to find some silver in the wreckage.

"Dan! I'm heading back!"

His brother's head poked into the room a moment later, eyeing the basket in his arms, "Find something?"

"Just some sewing stuff… for the girls."

"Alright, we won't be far behind you. We may have to come back with some pack-donkeys."

For what? All the silver they were finding? Joseph nodded but hid his skepticism. Maybe Dan was thinking of trying to haul off the furniture. He shook his head at the absurd possibility as he went out into the street.

It was quiet now, deathly so. The wails were gone, leaving just a few midday songs of birds, twined together with the whistle of the wind breezing down the valley and across the flat rooftops.

Joseph made for the gate but hesitated three houses down the narrow street. A sudden crash tore through the noon quiet, a noise like a pot shattering. Two houses back he would have chalked it up to Dan being careless, but here the door to the house was closed and…

He swallowed and set aside the basket, clutching his spear with both hands. His entire body tensed.

Might be nothing, he told himself. Someone's cat prowling a high shelf for scraps. Then he noticed a bloody smear on the door frame.

Or not.

His heart was pounding like he'd just run a race as he lowered his spear and tapped at the door.

The door didn't make a sound as it slid open just a hair. Waiting a few heartbeats in the stillness, he caught noises like feet scraping the floor within. Joseph sucked in a nervous breath.

Then he threw his weight against the door, and swept inside, spear leveled, to find… a girl?

She was about his own age, frozen in place with haunted, puffy red eyes, and a bulky pack looped around her shoulder. The front of her tan dress was drenched a bloody scarlet, and for a heartbeat the two locked eyes.

"Amaleigh?" Joseph didn't know many of the girls of the city, but he'd seen Dinah's friends enough times to recognize her.

His words broke whatever spell hung between them. Amaleigh dropped her pack and bolted for a spear leaned near the wall, gripping it with shaky hands. "Joseph, just leave."

Joseph looked around the room, his eyes going to the pieced together travel pack at her feet, then to a bloody motionless figure in the corner. Another familiar face, her brother, Lakan. "Amaleigh," he didn't budge, "you won't survive out there alone. There are bears, lions, and if they don't get you, someone else will."

"And that's different from this how?"

Joseph didn't have a good answer for that and looking at the desperation in her eyes he suddenly wasn't so sure of himself.

"Please," Amaleigh begged. "They're all dead. I just want to go."

Joseph hesitated, and for an instant he might almost have let her leave… but he never had the chance.

"Well, what's this?" Dan's voice interrupted from the doorway. "You found yourself a girl, Joseph?"

Joseph glanced back at both his half-brothers, watching him with twinkles of amusement in their eyes.

"A feisty girl." Naphtali added.

Whatever possibilities that might have hung between him and Amaleigh vanished like mist in the sun. He could see from the way her lips tightened that she knew it too.

"Don't touch me." She lowered her spear-point to force him back and Joseph struck, hard.

He batted her spear aside, rushed in close, and in the blink of an eye Amaleigh was pinned against the back wall. "Let me go!" she screamed, tears in her voice. "You bastard, let me go!"

The girl fought like a cornered cat, her nails raked at his cheek, and her foot hammered hard at his shin. Their faces hovering just inches apart, Joseph tried to pin her wrists against the wall, but Amaleigh was slippery. Her knee lashed up as if she was aiming for his groin. It jarred hard against his thigh, and feeling the fight slipping away, Joseph snapped his elbow up.

A stab of agony spiking down his arm, and somewhere nearby he heard Amaleigh scream.

Joseph stumbled back, clutching his elbow and trying not to bite his tongue against the pain.

Amaleigh dropped.

It took a good five heartbeats for the pain to clear enough for Joseph to start paying attention again. But when he did, Amaleigh was slumped on the ground, sobbing, both hands pressed against her cheek.

Still wincing at the stabbing pain in his elbow, Joseph kicked away both their discarded spears. His fingers touched at his cheek where her nails had gouged him, and he hissed at the sting, as they came away streaked with crimson.

For a second, he was afraid she might come at him again. But down at his feet, Amaleigh was curled up, like all the fight in her was gone, leaving just a horrible, agonizing emptiness.

"You lying bastards," she half moaned, half screamed through her tears. "You murdered them all."

Massaging at his elbow, Joseph stared a long moment, and… he didn't know what to do.

For some reason, his mind went straight to all the times he'd been on the losing end of a fight and ended up on the ground, trying not to cry against the pain. He felt a sickening lump gathering in his stomach, and suddenly found himself wishing he'd never seen her at all.

He glanced back at Dan, like the older boy might know what to do with the weeping girl, but his half-brother just shrugged. For a moment that seemed to stretch into forever, Joseph just stood there, lost, and feeling about as valiant as a slug.

Chapter 11
Broken Threads

Walking back to camp a half hour later, Joseph found himself wishing the day could be over already. Wishing he could go to sleep and not have to wonder what happened next, not have to see the shattered girl plodding a few paces in front of him. Not have to feel like he did.

It wasn't far back to camp from the city, but as they got close, he felt he had to say… something, anything to break through the stony nothingness that hung between them. Everything he could imagine saying sounded stupid in his own head, but eventually something forced its way out.

"I'm sorry… about your brother," Joseph said in a small, quiet voice. "I always liked him. If he was out in the fields and saw the goats scatter, he'd come help round them up. I always appreciated it."

A few paces in front of him, holding the woven basket of thread, needles and dye in her hands, Amaleigh didn't answer. She didn't speak at all.

She hadn't said a word since they'd left. After she'd finally run out of tears, she'd meekly picked up the basket when he'd said to and walked, one foot in front of the other, her eyes staring numbly at the dirt path.

An instinct deep down kept prompting him to ask if she was alright, but… well, obviously she wasn't. Something told Joseph that the question was more cruel than kind at this point.

Instead he found himself staring at the bronze tipped spear in his own hands, a part of him marveling at the absurdity of the whole affair. He'd been able to carry the basket fine on his own, but now here they were, her carrying the basket and him standing with a razor point to her back. He wasn't quite sure how this was better for any of them.

A dozen steps behind, his two half-brothers were apparently feeling less circumspect. They joked as they walked, a crude humor that made him wish Amaleigh wasn't here at all.

The two had managed to load themselves and Amaleigh down with perhaps the most useless looted trash they could have found. An armful of men's tunics, several bulky wineskins, and a delicately embroidered quilt that they'd probably end up ruining. About the only sensible thing they'd done was fold the quilt in Amaleigh's basket where it wouldn't get dragged through the dirt.

The whole camp was in even more of an uproar than when they'd left. People shouted over the bleats of goats as women bustled from tent to tent. Meanwhile, every freeman he saw was carrying either a spear or a bow. In the center of it all, the oval clearing surrounded by the ring of tents, sat a forlorn group of maybe seventy women and little children.

The survivors.

Joseph could only look at them for a moment. Then the awfulness of it all sank in, and he glanced away with a mumbled curse. Behind, he noticed even Dan and Naphtali's crass joshing had died away.

He nudged Amaleigh left with his spear-haft. If he could leave the basket at Myrrha's tent, he could leave and–

"Joseph!" Myrrha's alto voice cut through the jumbled noise of camp, and he twisted his neck to see her weaving through the crowd.

"Joseph, are you okay? Levi said…" Myrrha's voice faltered in her throat when she saw his prisoner.

While he and his brothers had been searching for silver, Myrrha looked like she'd been through a war all her own. She was carrying a roll of linen bandages, her brown hair messy and her expression haggard. Her pale arms were smudged with blood, and several crimson patches stained her tan work dress.

For an instant Myrrha stared, eyes wide, before a single word slipped out. "Amaleigh?"

The girl looked up but didn't seem to recognize Myrrha, which… why would she? If they'd ever met, Myrrha would have just been Dinah's nobody servant girl.

Myrrha's eyes shot straight to him though. "Joseph, what's going on?"

Joseph wanted to say he didn't know. Tell her that the world had turned upside-down on him since this morning, and he was just trying to keep up.

Instead what slipped out was, "We found her hiding in town."

Myrrha's gaze lingered a second on the battered girl, her expression souring at the dried blood beneath her nose and the massive bruise gathering above her cheek. When Myrrha spoke, her voice was heavy with disgust and disbelief, "Joseph, what did you do?"

Joseph frowned, not in the mood for another fight. "She had a spear, okay. I was just–"

"So you beat her?" Myrrha snapped, angry. Her eyes flickered to his two half-brothers, both watching, amused, "All three of you, I guess? Were you all very *proud* of yourselves afterwards?"

Naphtali's expression darkened. "Watch your mouth, Myrrha.".

"Yeah," she sneered, pointedly shooting Amaleigh's bloodied face another side glance, "I guess I'd better."

"Myrrha, not right now," Joseph said.

"Or what?" she fired right back, a look on her face like she barely even recognized him. "You're going to beat me too? Is that it?"

That stung. Of course he wouldn't. She knew that. And her throwing it in his face like that hurt.

"What's your problem?" Joseph demanded.

"My *problem*?" She gave a sarcastic wave like he'd asked what color the sky was. "Look around Joseph. Half the city is dead, I don't know if Dinah will ever be back to the way she was, Samas and I just spent all morning bandaging up people with no end in sight. And to cap it off, I just had to explain to a little girl that she never gets to see her dad again." Myrrha's voice wavered at that last bit. "Then I discover you've been right there doing your part to ruin lives too."

"That's not true," Joseph snapped, his temper slipping.

"Really?" Myrrha gestured to his recently captured slave girl. "Then I guess Amaleigh's free to go?"

"That's not how it works."

"Oh, and that makes it right?" Myrrha fumed, her expression hovering between raw fury and tears. "I suppose you believe Reuben's dung heap of a lie that you're *helping* too."

"No!" he roared back, as the last threads still holding his frustration in check finally frayed. "I don't! But this is how things are."

"Easy for you to say when you're holding the spear."

As she spoke, it finally struck home what Myrrha was so upset about. Not just today or tomorrow or Amaleigh, the town, Simeon… any of that. He could glimpse it in her eyes, hiding behind all the hurt and rage. The enormous, silent canyon that had hovered between them since as long as they'd known each other. "I'm sorry, okay?" The words slipped out before he could realize, things he imagined saying a hundred times but had never known how. "I'm sorry you're a slave and it has to be like this. I'm sorry you couldn't stay in Attica," he swallowed hard. "I'm sorry you never got to know your dad." Joseph sighed, "Myrrha, I wish it was different. But I can't fix that."

For a heartbeat the words hung in the space between them, a look on Myrrha's face like she'd been slapped. Standing there, Joseph couldn't guess what side of the knife edge he'd landed on. Somewhere between ruining everything and uttering something he should have said a long time ago.

Myrrha opened her mouth, but Naphtali's obnoxiously loud voice picked the worst possible moment to interrupt. "By the way, Myrrha, you're going to have to fix this quilt. It has a hole and I'm not giving Mom…"

"*Šiānu bêšu!*"

Myrrha snapped out the obscenity. Then froze, her face turning deathly pale as she realized what she'd just said, and to whom.

Naphtali tossed the quilt back in the basket and strolled towards her with a grim smirk. "I warned you Myrrha, but I guess a lesson might help remind–"

Joseph blinked–

He still remembered the one time Myrrha had been beaten, more than just a swat from her mom. They'd been stealing Leah's dresses off the drying line so Myrrha could sew the sleeves together.

It had been pretty funny, right until Nashu stumbled over them hiding up in the trees and hauled them both back. Joseph had gotten a tongue lashing, but in spite of his pleading, Myrrha hadn't been so lucky. He still remembered the terrified *in too deep* look on her face, and her hurt, humiliated sobs afterwards. He also remembered that he'd spent the rest of the day trying to cheer her up.

Naphtali stepped closer, and Joseph blanked. His whole world jumped three beats ahead.

When he could see again, there was a stabbing pain in his right hand like he'd just punched a knife. Myrrha was staring at him in shock, and down at his feet, Naphtali was sprawled on the ground, clutching his face and sputtering curses. "You son of a goat! I'll have you–"

"Stop it!" Dan shoved Joseph back a pace. "Both of you." He grabbed Naphtali as his brother scrambled to his feet and fairly hurled himself into the fight. "NOT… RIGHT… NOW!" Dan had to bodily haul Naphtali back.

"You're going to pay for that!" Naphtali warned, breathing hard.

Not today he wasn't. Joseph stared down his half-brother and resisted the urge to shake out his aching knuckles until Dan calmed Naphtali down enough for the two to take their loot and go.

He waited until they left, before finally massaging his hand with a sharp hiss of pain. "Myrrha I…"

He turned back but his friend wasn't there. She had knelt down beside Amaleigh, who'd been watching the whole thing and seemed more terrified than ever.

Myrrha looked back, and for an instant their eyes met, a confusion etched in hers like… like… she didn't know what it meant. Maybe he didn't either.

She turned her focus back to Amaleigh, helping the girl up, and picking up the basket herself. "Come on, I can look you over, make sure you're alright. We'll find you someplace to sleep."

The two girls left without so much as a goodbye. Joseph looked around, only to realize he was alone, frustrated and not sure what he was supposed to do.

He wanted to scream, but he couldn't. Not in camp. Across the circle of tents, he heard his dad's angry roar cut through the muddle of other voices. Joseph looked over to see him shouting at Simeon and Levi, "You fools, do you have any idea what you've done? You have ruined me! You've made me stink among all the people…"

Joseph turned away and barely heard the rest. Instead the words echoed in his head, what had he done? Somehow the only brothers he might have counted as friends now hated him. Myrrha didn't seem to want anything to do with him. And now that he thought about it, he hadn't even mentioned the dye he'd gotten for her, the thing that had sucked him into this disaster in the first place.

He tried to hide a stab of anger in his gut, suddenly wishing he could go back and shatter that stupid clay pot with all its blue powder.

The rest of his dad's words ran though his mind: *You have ruined me.*

Yeah, that felt accurate.

Chapter 12
Veiled Stars

Thunder cracked on the horizon as Joseph helped herd what he hoped was the last of the cattle into pens near their camp.

Spending the whole day rounding up stray animals on foot had left him bone tired, but with a gathering shadow looming over the valley, he didn't really have a choice. Besides, it was better than having to think about everything else.

Moving close, he gave one of the creatures a swift *whack* with his staff. The hesitant lead cow finally took a few tepid steps into the pen, deciding maybe it wasn't so bad after all, and the other twelve followed in a rush. Joseph finally allowed his staff to drop, and turned to go, leaving Issachar to get the gate.

His rough plan was to get back to his tent, tell everyone to leave him alone, and pass out until morning. Hopefully his problems would look a little more manageable then.

He paused when he saw his dad though, sitting off alone in front of the piled stone altar. His dad didn't move, even as the wind started to pick up and the sun sank down behind the clouds to the west, plunging the valley into a deepening bluish dusk.

"Dad?" Joseph walked up behind him, not sure what to say. He knew his dad wasn't happy about what had happened and–

"You're wanting an answer too, Joseph?" his father asked without even turning, eyes focused on the altar stones.

"Huh?"

His dad finally did turn at hearing his confusion and nodded him to sit. A stiff gust of wind whipped at his tunic. When it passed, Dad finally spoke. "Reuben and Simeon both want to occupy the city and lay in provisions for a siege."

A siege? After today Joseph wanted nothing to do with the city. He'd be fine never seeing it again. Just the thought of being holed up in there while an army bent on killing them camped outside was enough to twist his stomach.

"So, you believe they'll come for revenge?"

"The Hivites at least, yes. Probably also Jericho, Luz, Jebus, Megiddo, Shiloh." His father didn't bother to complete the list. "Hamor was a man of great repute and many friends. Your brothers have made none by killing him."

The news alone was grim, but his dad's dispassionate delivery somehow made it worse. Like that was just how the stones fell, and there wasn't anything they could do about it. Joseph hadn't paid much attention during the, 'you idiots, you've killed us all' talk earlier, but seeing it now, he started to understand why his father had been so keen *not* to fight. Turned out it was a lot easier to start a war than to end one.

"What about Uncle Esau in Seir?" Joseph asked, hopeful. He'd only met his uncle once, when he was little, but he still remembered. "He had a mighty army."

From the look on his dad's face, that was the wrong thing to say. Like there was a lot more between them than Joseph knew. "I… would not count on your uncle to come die for us. He might, but after what Simeon and Levi did, maybe not. Perhaps if things had been different, years ago…" Dad's voice trailed off.

In the silence that followed Joseph had only one question, "So then, what do we do?"

His dad kept staring at the altar, as though it might provide some miraculous answer, but in the end he shook his head. "I don't know," Jacob sighed, his grim tone mellowing some, even as a sharp crack of thunder sounded behind them, closer now. "You should get some sleep, Joseph."

The light was fading fast, and Joseph didn't need a second urging to go to bed. He stood to go but hesitated, noticing his dad still didn't move. "Aren't you coming?"

"I'll be along," his father said, unconcerned.

Joseph glanced back towards the wall of dark clouds backlit by the falling sun, catching a stab of lightning over the far hills. "There's a storm coming."

His dad nodded but still didn't move, a humorless smile playing across his face. "Indeed."

***

Joseph jolted awake to a deafening boom. A sharp crash split the air, followed by lingering cracks, like the rumbling aftershocks of a landslide.

It was pitch black in the tent, with only the constant howl of the wind, and the spatter of rain as it lashed against the goat-hide walls. Outside, another shrieking blast of wind battered the shelter until Joseph could almost hear the tentpoles straining to hold back the elements.

Abruptly the howling wind faded, gathering itself for a renewed effort. Overhead came another thunderous crack, and the tempest whistled back like a raging banshee. Only this time, it was accompanied by the sharp snap of hide flapping back and forth in the wind and a spray of dampness on Joseph's face.

In the gloom of the tent, Joseph couldn't see much, but outside a flash of lightning suddenly bathed the whole valley in an instant of bluish-white. When it did, Joseph saw.

One of the tent corners had jerked loose. Normally the whole perimeter was weighed down by heavy rocks, but pummeled by the relentless wind, it must have slipped free. Struggling in the blackness, he crawled over to the corner, trying to hold it down, even as another bolt of lightning strobed outside. After a moment fighting the wet leather, his night tunic was soaked with rain spray, and the instant he let go, the hide slipped free with a whip-crack.

Letting out a frustrated groan, Joseph rested his head on his palm for a heartbeat, before deciding there was nothing else for it. He couldn't ask Mom to fix it, she needed her sleep for the baby. But if he just left it, the rest of the wall could slip loose and the whole tent could blow away.

He had to go outside.

He fought a moment with the tent flap, his fingers fumbling at the knots that laced it up, before finally pulling them free. Fortunately, the flap was on the upwind side, so it wasn't instantly blown inwards. But as he undid the cord and found himself staring at a curtain of rain, if anything the storm seemed to intensify.

The thunder grew deep and loud until it sent a shudder down his spine, and the brilliant echoes of lightning came closer together. Stumbling outside into the mud and blinding rain, he felt his way around the tent, more by instinct than sight. He'd walked these same few steps for most of his life. When another flash did provide illumination, he found himself soaked and shivering, but right where he needed to be.

He spent another awful moment groping in the dark for the loose corner. The wind wailed in his ears while rainwater trickled down his forehead into his eyes. His hands sank into the cold mud as he tried to hold down the leather corner. It felt like forever scrambling in the miserable soaking darkness, punctuated only by thunderpeals and flashes of silver light that washed the valley. Finally though, holding down the tent with one foot, he fought the heavy stone back into place, pinning the goat hide to the mucky ground, the tent secured.

Relieved, freezing cold and covered in mud, he turned to bumble his way back inside. But when he did, another bolt of jagged white lashed down, no further than the other edge of camp. In the ear pounding afterglow, Joseph blinked past the water in his eyes to see a small figure still bowed before his family's altar. "Dad?"

Amid the cacophony of the storm, he wasn't sure if the word came out as a whisper or a shout. But an instant later, he called as loud as he could, "Dad!"

His father looked as though he hadn't moved in the hours since Joseph had seen him. All around him the rain spattered down, swirling and billowing in the air like waves of mist swept before a gale.

Stumbling towards him, Joseph wasn't quite sure what his plan was, when another blast of white slammed into the earth, not ten paces from his dad. It pulsed out a blinding starburst and a crack like a whole forest being felled at a stroke.

Joseph blinked, shielding his eyes as more stabs of sky-fire ringed the ground around his father, and overhead a roar shuddered even the ground itself.

When he did wince his eyes open, what he saw was… the wind and rain had twisted into a vortex around his dad. The lightning still rained down across the camp, but the noise seemed dim and faraway. For a moment the rumble of thunder resolved itself into… into a Voice.

Joseph felt that he should know the words. Like it was a language he'd heard before but couldn't quite remember. Even so, he stared, watching his dad, until at last the words, whatever they meant, faded back into the roar of thunder, and the cyclone of wind and water collapsed.

Slowly his father stood, whatever business he'd had at the altar finally done. Dad trudged back towards his tent, seemingly unconcerned with the raging storm. Joseph watched for a long moment, before the water dripping in his eyes and the rain pelting him like pebbles forced him to look away.

Another burst of wind rushed through the darkness, and Joseph shielded his face as he stumbled back around to the lee of the tent. The wind slackened a little as he knelt down to crawl inside. He didn't pause until he finished tying down the tent-flap. But with the storm locked away outside, the questions came rushing back.

What was that? He'd seen storms, lightning, thunder, all of it before, but not that. And his dad had just seemed so… calm afterwards.

Joseph wasted a few moments trying to wipe the mud off his hands and arms, but in the dark, he mostly just managed to smear it around a bit more. Eventually he gave up, felt his way back over to the mat he'd been sleeping on, and huddled down beneath his blanket, trying to stay warm. Whatever. They could clean it in the morning. That was why they had servants.

A part of him chuckled. Myrrha would have thrown a fit it he'd said that aloud, but… it was true, and–

Just the name brought the memory of all his other problems rushing back. Enough to push aside the… the whatever that was, that he'd just witnessed.

Joseph lay there a while, the wind still shrieking outside, but not so loud as before. Even when he tried not to, he found himself mulling through things in his head, questions he didn't have answers for. Behind it all hovered a single looming enigma, a shadow he didn't want to look at for fear it might just be real. It was the last thing to scamper through his mind as he drifted on the edge of sleep.

What *had* he seen in the storm?

Chapter 13
Small gods

By morning the storm had passed. The sun crept back out to drench the world in a muggy haze, while the entire camp transformed into a frenzied hive of activity.

"Joseph," he looked up from packing to see his mom hesitating, two small statuettes in her hands. For a moment she bit at her lip, staring at one, the polished black stone figurine of a seated man. Finally, she let out a long, reluctant sigh. "Take them."

She struggled a moment to stand with her pregnant belly, but finally forced herself upright. She took two steps over, offering him both figures.

"Huh?" Joseph stared for a second, not really sure why he would want them. They were pretty, each just the right size to sit in his cupped hands, intricately carved in shapes like a man and woman and both with a polished luster like gleaming onyx. That said, he didn't really have a use for them and...

"Take them," his mom insisted, more forceful this time.

"What is–"

"Just leave them outside your father's tent," she said without much explanation.

Oh, it took a few heartbeats longer than it probably should have, but Joseph finally realized what the black statuettes were. He stared a long moment at the little gods in his mom's hands, silently wondering where in the world she'd gotten the gleaming idols. Finally

though, he accepted them, his mind flashing back to
earlier that morning.

***

"We are leaving." Jacob said in a voice that carried
across the assembled crowd near his tent. Except for the
newest additions to their camp from the city, everyone
was there– Joseph's brothers, the herdsmen, most of the
servants. He'd caught Myrrha and her mom earlier
amid the sea of familiar faces. All of them wondering
what they were supposed to do now that the whole
world was coming for them. And after the windstorm
last night, everyone was on edge.

It had nearly blown away at least two tents. In the
dawn light, he could see cracked limbs hanging off
trees while shattered branches with the leaves still fresh
and green were scattered across the grass. More than a
few people had shadows under their eyes from the long
night. Although, somehow, almost miraculously, the
animals hadn't kicked their pens apart and scattered.
That was about the only thing that had gone well
though.

Up near the front, Reuben didn't look happy at the
pronouncement. "Why leave?" he demanded, the
challenge hanging in the still morning air. "Why should
we abandon the city?"

"Because we have somewhere else to be," Jacob
said, a flinty hardness in his voice like he would brook
no dispute.

"And what about the Canaanites?" Levi voiced the
question that Joseph guessed everyone else must have
been thinking. "When they come, we stand a better
chance fighting behind the walls than strung out on the
road. How–"

"We're done fighting." Jacob cut him off, his voice
sharp and a look in his eyes like they could talk about
this later, when the whole camp *wasn't* watching.

92

"But—"

"I said *we are done*." Joseph's dad didn't give them another opening. He took a deep breath and raised his voice. "I have no intention of staying here to die at the hands of the Hivites, whether in the field or in the city. If some of you disagree," he shot a warning glare at Reuben, Levi and a heavily bandaged Simeon near the front, "then the city is open to you. Otherwise, we are leaving this forsaken place and going somewhere we will be safe." Jacob glanced around, like he was daring someone to take him up on the offer as he continued. "Get rid of the foreign gods that are among you. Purify yourselves and change your clothes. We must get up and go to Bethel. I will build an altar there to the God who answered me in the day of my distress. He has been with me everywhere I have gone." Jacob's voice hesitated a heartbeat. "He will not abandon us now."

A murmur rippled through the crowd at his words. For his part Joseph felt a nervous lump gathering in his stomach. He had heard of Bethel. His father had talked about it on occasion, the House of God. It was somewhere south, he wanted to say. But he wasn't sure what going there was supposed to do. It felt like running except... the memories from the storm the night before were still etched in his mind. The impossible voice that had swelled out of the thunder, and his dad had looked so calm after hearing it, even despite the gale.

It was enough to make Joseph wonder.

From behind them though came a different sort of question. "What do you mean by foreign gods?" a worried voice called out from the back of the crowd.

"I mean everything," Jacob declared bluntly. "Your idols, your rings, your talismans. If it is not holy to The Lord God, then it must be removed. We are going to the House of God, and we will not bring our petty charms with us."

He looked out across the crowd, even as Joseph heard a quiet grumbling crop up in several places behind him. For an instant he thought it might be people worried about just leaving, but then he caught a fragment of a whisper back in the crowd, "…just wants it for himself. I'd bet he…"

The real objection clicked in Joseph's head. At nearly the same instant his dad's face hardened to a disappointed frown, his voice rising over the ripple of objections. "This is not about *money*." He uttered the word with disdain in his voice. "For anyone who hasn't realized, we recently have silver and livestock in great abundance. If your gods are of such great value, come talk and I can recompense you a fair price."

His eyes roved across the crowd who had suddenly grown quiet at the words. "You have until noon today, after that your idols are between you and God." He paused a long second, "I assure you, keeping them would not be wise."

***

Joseph found the front of his dad's tent thrown wide open, his father sitting next to a mixed pile of idols, copper wrought trinkets and little sacred earrings. He walked up just as Nashu was leaving with a small drawstring bag in one hand that clunked with bits of silver.

Stooping to duck under the awning, Joseph saw his father setting aside a foot-long, elaborate, bronze statue of a bull with exaggerated horns.

"Joseph, what are…" He father looked up to greet him but froze when he saw the little statues in his hands. His voice turned breathless, "Where did you get those?"

"Mom had them," Joseph stammered, trying to sort out what his dad's strange response meant. "She wanted uhh…"

Joseph had a hard time making the right words come out. He finally just handed over both carved statues. "Here."

Jacob held one for a moment, eyes fixed on it and a look on his face like it had transported him somewhere far away. "Do you know what these are, Joseph?"

"A… statue of a little man… god… thing?"

His dad chuckled and added the idols to the rest of the pile. "Where is the sun?"

Joseph didn't really need to check. He'd noted the sun on the way over, mostly out of habit. Even so, he glanced back out the front of the low awning, where he could instantly tell the time by the short stubby shadows that huddled at the base of a few tents. "Almost midday."

His dad nodded, wordlessly considering the news for a moment, before pushing himself to his feet, and walking out into the bright day with only a hint of a limp. "Would anyone else like to take my offer!" he called across the camp.

Jacob waited a long moment, but when no one answered he turned back. "Joseph, could you get a few shovels, then hook up a cart and a donkey and bring them here."

Joseph wasn't sure what his dad intended, but he nodded anyway.

After a quick raid on their pile of tools, it was the work of only a few minutes to harness a donkey to a simple two-wheeled wooden cart. In less time than it took to eat lunch he was back, helping as his dad unceremoniously loaded the pile of precious things into the back of the cart.

They got more than a few strange looks as they worked, but apparently everyone was satisfied with whatever compensation they'd gotten. In a short while, his dad was leading the donkey away from camp, taking the path back towards the ruined city. Joseph followed close behind, twirling a staff in case he needed to give the donkey a prod.

He couldn't help eyeing the pile of discarded idols as he walked. It was an eclectic collection, valuable as well– carved stone and wood figurines, gleaming bronze and copper earrings with a few engraved silver talismans thrown in.

Joseph's eyes lingered on Nashu's strange bull creature. "So is this… a god?" He picked up the statuette, running a finger over the delicately carved details.

His father looked back. "It's Kaphtorian, I don't believe it's a god itself, more of a token. Nashu said it represented the bull from the sea. I didn't ask what it meant. Doesn't really matter anyway." He walked a few more paces in quiet before adding, "The Egyptians do worship bulls though. And Dhra, from what he's said, in his home they have sacred white cows with humps like camels."

Joseph stared at the strange bull for a moment, before tossing it back onto the pile and picking one of his mom's onyx figurines out instead. "And what about this?" He held it up, the statue looking like a little squat man

His father only had to glance back. "Your mother didn't tell you what it was?"

Joseph shook his head, and Jacob let out a long sigh. For a moment Joseph hung on edge, certain that his dad wouldn't say, but finally, "I didn't know she had them, but they belonged to your grandfather, Laban."

Joseph nearly missed a step. He had maybe two or three flickering memories of his grandfather, a bearded man with traces of white in his hair who always seemed to tower up over him like a giant. One was them walking near Harran, watching a caravan while Laban pointed out the beehive shaped huts of the city and explained who lived in each. The other was sharper, his grandfather stalking towards them at the head of a troop of armed men, angry. Meanwhile his mom stood behind him, clutching his shoulder, her fingers digging painfully into his upper back.

"I'm guessing she stole them," his dad added.

Joseph frown, "Stole them?" And suddenly, like he'd found a stone just the right size to fit in among the rest, a half dozen other little stories about his grandfather snapped into clear focus. "Are these why grandfather came after us? When we tried to leave?"

Joseph might only have recalled snippets, but he'd heard the full story from Reuben and Simeon. Laban chasing them nearly to Canaan, and finally catching up with them a day or two north of here, armed and ready for a fight. How he'd torn the camp apart looking for… something.

His dad spoke, "There were… a lot of reasons your grandfather came after us." He glanced back at the little idol in Joseph's hands. "But that was certainly one." He paused, his expression turning more amused, "That said, I'm not sure how your mother hid them. I recall Laban being irritatingly thorough when he went hunting for them."

Joseph filed that away as a question to ask his mom later. He spent another moment looking at the small idol before setting it back in the cart, a part of him marveling in amazement. Why had Uncle Laban chased them all the way from Harran over such a little thing? For that matter, why had Mom stolen it?

They were still heading towards the ruined city, but before they came too close, his dad silently turned off to the right, the cart bumping over tufts of grass in the valley. His dad wasn't talking much. Joseph wasn't sure if it was just because he didn't have anything to say, or if the moment itself was a sort of solemn occasion. Even so, he felt more questions lingering in his throat, and when Joseph couldn't keep back his curiosity any longer one finally slipped out.

"Dad, where are we going?"

For several paces his dad didn't answer, and Joseph had the awful feeling he'd spoiled something special by talking. Finally, the answer came back in a single enigmatic sentence, his dad gesturing at all the idols in the cart. "To make an end of this."

Joseph had only been in the sacred grove of Moreh once, a long time ago, tagging along with Dan and Naphtali on a late-night adventure. Then, the towering oak had loomed like a dark, creaking wraith in the night.

Now, forcing his way through the thick green of terebinth branches and dragging on the donkey's harness to get it to follow, he found the grove strangely calm. The huge oak of Moreh still rose towards the sky, but in the light of day it seemed less ominous and solemn, almost a curiosity with its gigantic drooping limbs.

Strolling to a spot beneath the shade of the oak, his dad kicked at the ground with one foot like he was marking a spot. "This should do." He grabbed both shovels from the cart and tossed one to Joseph. "We'll dig here."

Joseph didn't mind digging. The soil was soft and loamy after the rain, with none of the usual rocks that would crack the wooden scoops. But it wasn't until his fourth shovel of dark earth that it finally registered what they were doing. He glanced at the cart, his mouth dropping open in disbelief.

"We're burying all this?"

His dad's eyes flicked up to meet his for a moment, utterly unconcerned, before focusing back on deepening their small hole. "We are."

"But–" Joseph wasn't even sure where to begin, "Dad, we just spent how much silver buying all this and you're going to…?"

Joseph's voice trailed off.

What were they doing?

"We could at least melt down the metal. The bronze alone would be worth something."

His dad gave a heavy sigh and stood leaning on his shovel. "Joseph, it's not about the silver."

"Then why did we just spend so much buying all this?" Joseph insisted. "How does that make any–"

"*We?*" His dad cut him off with raised eyebrows. "*We* did not spend anything. *I* made the decision."

Joseph crossed his arms, *we, I, whatever*. It might still belong to his dad, but Joseph couldn't escape the sense that it was a little bit his business too. He glanced at the pile of valuables in the cart. "Dad, why would you waste silver on all this if you're just going to throw it away?"

His dad's fingers rapped at the shaft of his shovel. "Because no one would understand otherwise," he finally said. "If I'd just tried to take it all, I've have a revolt on my hands. People would think I meant to hoard it or…" He frowned, "I suppose I shouldn't be so hard on them. When all you have is a cloak, the cloak means a great deal. It's asking a lot."

Yeah, a lot of silver, Joseph thought, reluctantly scooping another shovel full of dirt. Apparently, he wasn't doing a good job hiding his displeasure though.

Walking over to the cart, his dad stared at the pile of valuables for a moment. "You disagree?"

Yeah, he disagreed. Joseph didn't say it though. He got the sense he wouldn't change his father's mind.

His mind was still stuck on the, *no one would understand* part though. Was that why Dad had asked him to come at all, because he thought he might? Joseph knew Reuben or Simeon would still be fighting to keep everything. Some of the others might have gone along with it, just to come back later and dig it all up. Maybe this was Dad trusting him, he realized. And when he did, he wanted to understand.

"Is this about what happened last night?" Joseph asked, taking another shovel scoop. "In the storm?"

Jacob froze, his demeanor suddenly on edge. "You heard the Voice too?"

"I heard…" Joseph had to think on that, even now, he wasn't entirely sure himself and just recalling the surreal scene left him uncertain. "I heard something."

He hesitated, trying to puzzle out the thoughtful look on his dad's face, not sure if it was his place to ask more. Finally though, he did. "Dad, why were you even out there in the storm?"

His dad took a few more shovels of soil before replying. "Waiting. For answers."

Joseph almost asked if he'd found any, but maybe he didn't need to. He'd heard the voice from the storm, and now they were off to Bethel, all the while leaving a treasure in bronze, copper and silver behind. Clearly the world was changing.

The two dug in silence for a few more minutes, his shovel cutting into the moist earth before his dad finally seemed to decide it was enough. "This should do." He pulled forward the donkey, so the cart was alongside the hole and began depositing the menagerie of gods and trinkets into the dirt.

Deep down, Joseph still winced at seeing so many precious talismans just left to rot, but Dad caught his eye. "These are small things," Jacob insisted. "Very small, compared to God."

Joseph wasn't quite so sure. But then again, certainly they were small compared to… whatever the voice had been.

Staring at the pile of little idols, he noticed one he recognized and pulled it out. A finely carved wooden statuette of a woman in a long robe with a spear in one hand and an owl perched upon the other. Myrrha's… or well, her mom's. Athena Polias, the name sprang to mind. She'd shown it to him one day when they'd both been younger. She'd been teaching him some of her mom's native language as a sort of code. When he'd asked her what Attica was like, she'd dug it out to show him.

The code part hadn't really worked, since apparently Nashu spoke Mycenaean better than both of them. Still, it was nice to remember a time when things weren't so complicated.

Holding the figurine in his hand for a moment, Joseph took one final look before stooping down to gently set it in the hole alongside all the others.

Hopefully his dad was right about this.

Chapter 14
The Long March

Myrrha still wasn't talking to him.

Not that they'd had a whole lot of chances. In between burying the idols the prior day, packing up his mom's tent, loading, literally, stacks of flaxen floormats onto camels and somehow compressing his entire life down into a bundle that fit in his arms, Joseph hadn't had much time to do anything besides work, let alone wonder about her.

Now that they were walking though, he found himself constantly dwelling on it. It was either that, or start obsessing like Reuben about the horde of avenging Canaanites ready to swoop down on them in the exposed valley. Which… given their current lumbering crawl, if that really was the case, then they were all dead, regardless of how much they panicked. At least Reuben could have had the courtesy to save his breath and stop pestering everyone to hurry up.

Trudging along near the middle of the column, Joseph held the reins to his mom's camel as it took one, lazy, camel speed step after another. Next to him Grandma Dede and his mom were talking about something to do with the sun feeling hotter than usual. His eyes were focused up ahead though, staring at Myrrha, her brown hair tied back with a cream strip of linen while she led a donkey loaded down with rolled up tent bundles.

He might have gone on up to talk, except for who else was up there – Amaleigh. She was pulling along

Dinah's favorite camel, Olive. Dinah had picked her out as a calf, cried whenever anyone whacked the creature and eventually the camel had turned into the most spoiled, ornery animal they had. Which explained why Amaleigh was having to fight Olive just to keep their plodding pace.

After everything that had happened, he felt awkward enough with just Myrrha, let alone Amaleigh and Dinah, who still seemed to think of Amaleigh as more of a friend than a… slave?

That was probably the right word, but it felt strange using it to talk about people he'd known as free a few days before. Not for the first time, he found himself wishing Simeon and Levi could have just let things go, or at least… not caused all this.

"Joseph?" his mom's voice broke into his thoughts, and he glanced back to where she sat jostling at each plodding camel step.

"Huh?"

"Are you okay?" His mom leaned forward in her saddle.

"I… I'm fine," he managed to cover. "Just thinking."

His mom nodded, but still had an unconvinced frown. Before she probed more, her expression tightened, one hand falling to her swollen belly.

"Mom?" Joseph bit at his lip, "Is everything…?"

For a few long seconds she didn't answer, until finally seeming to notice him again. "It's nothing out of the ordinary," she forced a smile.

Right, Joseph sighed, and glanced at Dede, hoping for a hint. She just gave him her usual, half-amused, lazy stare and called him out right there. "Don't know why you'd think I know anything about having babies, Joseph," Dede mused loud enough to make his face redden. "Not sure if you noticed, but I never had much experience in the baby realm."

Joseph made a point to look… anywhere that *wasn't* his mom, but even so he could almost feel her gaze on the back of his head. "Joseph," his mom insisted, "I'm fine, really. Although, if you're feeling up to it, Deborah and I could both use a waterskin."

He wasted a second flagging over the closest person, who happened to be Tamarra, to hold the harness for a minute. It wasn't until he found the water skins that the irony of it all dawned on him.

The one thing they could all agree on, they were all *fine*.

It was midday before they reached the south end of the Ebal Vale. The long valley strung out behind them, a wide, familiar strip of verdant grass running off into the distance like an emerald river. Thick forests painted the hills to the east and west in a darker, foreboding green, and straight ahead, to the south, rose more forested highlands.

Slowly the valley necked down into The Narrows, a winding rocky path that rose into the rugged hills near Shiloh.

Even trying to keep the herds together, the animals were soon strung out. Joseph found himself near the middle of the column, using a spear instead of his normal staff to push along a flock of thirsty sheep already exhausted from the trek. The entire winding caravan would never be able to stop and water all together either, so eventually Joseph paused near a little pool, freshly filled with stormwater, to give the sheep a rest.

The lambs might have appreciated it, but Joseph found his gaze constantly searching the forest that loomed up the hills around them. Every wolf, lion and bear within twenty miles would probably be back in those trees, stalking them, waiting for a goat or a lamb to wander off. Even as he watched, a long mournful howl rose in the distance, the wolves gathering. All around him, weary sheep scrambled to their feet in alarm, and Joseph sighed, circling wide to round them up and herd them on. Time to go then.

The flock didn't really agree, and he had a hard fight to push them away from their water. It might have been better if the terrain wasn't so tough, and the pace wasn't so fast. Usually when they brought a flock through here, it was a small group of animals, and it took a leisurely two days. Now, he passed right by their usual stopping point, a rocky hill just off the path, marked by a thick stone overhang where they would all shelter for the night. There was usually a small rainwater pool in a nearby rocky basin. Except, as he passed by, Joseph saw the pool was gone, just dark, silty mud lingering at the bottom, where the animals had drunk it dry.

The sight just left him thirstier than before, even as his sheep set to bleating. They knew the pool was supposed to be there too and wanted to stop. But not today.

That evening they didn't so much make camp as just stopped walking when the sun began falling behind the western hills. It had taken hours, but the long procession had finally made it out of the Narrows down into the curve of the Lubban Valley. Laid out before them in the gathering darkness was a swath of fertile tranquility shadowed by the forested heights to either side. With more space, the endless train of animals began to reassemble, the chorus of distressed bleats and lows only growing quiet when they finally found a deep pond. But at least it was water.

The small village of farmers that called the valley home were gone. Their cluster of empty houses was stripped strangely bare of fresh bread and waterskins. However, several herdsmen quickly discovered bulky jugs of olive oil and wine sitting in a cooling cellar next to thick cuts of salted gazelle meat. Even a family of cats clung around the small granary, suffering some of the younger girls to pet them in trade for scraps of meat.

Somewhere between a hurried meal of hard bread and bedding the animals down, Joseph managed to secure one of the empty homes for his mom. But by the time she'd invited Bilhah, and about a dozen other maidservants inside for the night, Joseph somehow found himself sleeping outside. His back to the mud brick wall, he huddled down beneath two blankets against the chilly evening.

As night came, Joseph could see the glow from the fires of Shiloh, like a gigantic candle hidden from view behind a sloping hill. That would be tomorrow's problem. And it was a big problem.

Overhead the stars shone down, twinkling in the clear darkness, speckled like glowing sand across the sky. For a while the breezes whipped at his face. On glassy clear nights like this, it got cold fast, no matter what time of year it was. Soon he was rubbing at his chilly nose, even as one of the women inside took up a gentle snoring. Fortunately, compared to Dan's throaty wheezes, the snores were barely audible. Besides, he was used to sleeping outside. Way too much practice. It was easy really; the trick was just to be more tired than you were uncomfortable. Slowly his body crept across that line of exhaustion, until he finally slipped away into blackness.

***

The next morning Joseph stirred awake to find the sun peeking over the horizon and shining right in his face. He spent a moment stretching out the stiffness in his back, even as their impromptu camp rapidly morphed into a hive of activity. Fifty paces off, Reuben stalked through the bustle in a boiled-leather breastplate, spear in hand, barking out orders, in his *I'm important* voice. The shouts of herdsmen echoed everywhere, and nearby he saw his mom directing

106

Fannah to strap a tight rolled bundle onto the back of her camel.

She smiled when he wandered up. "There you are. I saved you some food." Mom rapidly produced several strips of dried jerky from a pouch.

Still a little drowsy, Joseph blinked in surprise. "Thanks."

He took a few tentative nibbles, at which point his stomach finally remembered he hadn't eaten dinner last night. Their jerky was usually lackluster at best, but this morning the salted meat tasted almost divine. He wolfed down the first two strips, watching as Levi and Judah both strode past, toting spears and outfitted in leather breastplates and armguards. Ready for a fight.

He glanced up at the tree-capped hill that hid Shiloh, sunlight streaming over it like a copper river. He took another nervous bite of jerky, finding it suddenly didn't taste quite as good as before. It was going to be a big day. A terrifyingly big day.

An hour later Joseph glanced up the hill at the high walls of Shiloh, barely two bowshots away. His grip tightened around his spear haft at all the faces staring back. He urged his flock of sheep onwards, wishing they could just be past the city already.

He would have preferred to go… any other way really. Unfortunately, if they wanted to get south, the Shiloh Pass was their only option. The thick scrub forests that carpeted the low hills to either side funneled their herds into the valley, right past the city. Now, even clumped together for safety, Joseph couldn't escape the awful foreboding that the gates were about to burst open. The men of Shiloh would flood down the hill in a hail of arrows and spears, and in short order their camp would meet the same fate as Shechem.

Already he could hear the shouts as they passed. "Keep on moving, you rats!" "Come to rob us too?" And the one that really stung. "Murderers!"

Off to his left, he spotted his dad standing near Reuben, Simeon and a few of the older servants, all with their eyes honed towards the city. He probably should have stayed with the sheep, but with Asher bringing up a herd of goats right behind, his flock would keep moving with or without him.

Joseph dropped out of the column.

He found his dad wearing a boiled leather breastplate, heavy war bow strung, and his spearpoint jabbed into the earth at his side. Reuben was talking, "There should be more of us here," he insisted. "If they come out now, we're scattered across the whole…"

"And who would drive the herds then?" Jacob interrupted in a strained tone, like this wasn't the first time they'd discussed this. "Reuben, if they come out to fight, it won't matter."

"Of course it will," Reuben snapped. "If we're armored and together we can–"

"They outnumber us and they'll range us from the hill," Jacob said in a voice like he was finished with the topic. "Together, apart, we die either way."

Fuming, Reuben turned to leave, and for a heartbeat Joseph met his older brother's gaze. In that instant Joseph had the strangest sense, like his older brother was sizing him up, deciding if *he* was the sort of help he'd been wanting. Then Reuben's face creased in a disappointed frown, and he brushed past with a foul temper and a curt, "What do you want?"

His dad managed a smile at seeing him though. "Joseph? Is everything alright?"

Joseph nodded but didn't leave, his eyes flicking from his dad to Simeon, Levi, Nashu, a burly herdsman named Michael, then up to the city on the hill above them. "What's uhh…"

Nashu shook his head, like he found the whole situation comical. "Oh, we're just standing around, looking intimidating and all," he said casually. "You can join us if you want. I suppose we need somebody to replace Reuben. Let *them,*" he nodded towards Shiloh, "know we won't be an easy fight."

Joseph frowned, "There's only five of you?" He wasn't sure how they were supposed to hold off an entire city.

Nashu just nodded. "Well, we can't have everyone standing here. They might realize they outnumber us. Best not to act too concerned, since we don't win a straight fight either way."

That… seemed like a not particularly brilliant way of looking at things. Before Joseph could ask his dad though, he caught a shout off to the left, and turned to see… people running *towards* Shiloh?

Two women and a little girl.

Dressed in simple work tunics it took him a heartbeat to recognize them, two of the older women they'd taken from the city. And then it clicked. They were running. Up and down the column came more shouts. Suddenly there were twenty, thirty, fifty of their new slaves all breaking in a chaotic mad scramble towards the walls of Shiloh.

Nearby, Nashu swore, and Joseph heard his dad's bellowing voice. "What the… SOMEONE STOP THEM!"

There were more screams and the sound of scuffles breaking out all along the column. Looking back, Joseph saw two herdsmen cutting off several young women who were still tangled up amid the animals. Most of them were too far gone though, and no one was going to be running *towards* the city to get them back.

"Dammit!" his father swore. "This is not…"

"Oh, I'll stop them," Simeon said, deadpan serious. He calmly unwound a thick leather sling from around his waist, dropped a stone in the pocket, and twirled it overhead to build up momentum.

He got three twirls before his dad jabbed a spear up into the sling's arc, the leather cords twisting around the spear haft in an instant. The stone snapped against the wooden haft with a sharp crack.

"What in Sheol are you doing!" Jacob demanded, staring at Simeon like he'd gone mad.

"Well, you wanted them to stop."

"Simeon, I want them back alive." Jacob shook his head and turned away, teeth gritted. "Are you trying to prove their point for them?" he asked, gesturing towards the city. "I'm sure a few dead women and children would do that nicely."

Already most of the escapees were barreling uphill almost beyond sling range. His dad might still be able to hit them with his war bow. The draw was so strong that really only he and Nashu could pull it. But his dad hadn't so much as laid an arrow on the string.

"Joseph, get back to the herd," he said tersely. "Tell them to hurry. We need to be away from Shiloh by the time they sort out that mess. If they do decide to seriously come after us, take your mother and run." He glanced over at Levi nearby, "Levi, that stands for you too. Get Leah and get out of here."

"But…" Joseph tried to object.

"Back to the herds," his father cut him off. "Remember, we need to move fast."

Reluctantly Joseph gave a nod. His sheep were far up ahead now, and he had to jog to catch up. "Joseph, what's happening?" Asher called as he passed.

"It's under control." Joseph shouted, "But we have to keep moving."

He found his sheep in disarray, a pack of lambs straying off, and spent a moment gathering them all back into a group. When he finally did look back, he saw all the people had vanished back into the city, the gates slamming shut behind them. There were still soldiers watching from the walls, but not as many now, like perhaps the sudden influx of refugees had thrown off whatever plans the people of Shiloh had been hatching. There were a few shouts, but they were getting far enough past that Joseph couldn't make them out over the bleats of his flock.

Just keep going, he murmured, shooing the sheep along, and following the curve of the valley where the rest of their caravan turned to continue off south. He kept looking back though, until Shiloh diminished in the distance.

The rest of the day felt like the march would never end. Even through the sweltering noon heat they moved at a grueling pace, up hills, down hills, through low patches, back up hills and close to trees.

He glimpsed a lioness once, a ways off, watching them. She stood motionless, probably calculating if her pride stood a chance at scoring a meal, before turning and silently padding back into the trees. Joseph could see the sheep flagging badly too. He'd spent enough time with them to know when they were just complaining and when they actually needed a rest. And right now, they were bleating their utter exhaustion.

They were getting close to Bethel though, moving out of the narrow valleys into more open plains to the south. As the sun slowly dropped past afternoon, Joseph found himself gripping his sling tight, tempted to whip off a stone. To the west he watched the silhouetted figure of a man retreat back behind the crest of a rocky hill, vanishing into the glare of evening. No doubt heading off to report on them.

"From Luz, probably," Nashu's voice interrupted.

Joseph started and spun to see their chief tracker wearing his usual mix of brown and dark green, his quiver casually slung across his back and a strung bow in one hand. Somehow, he'd walked up no more than a few feet behind him without making a sound.

"Should we go after him?" Joseph asked.

Nashu shook his head with a grin. "Now you're starting to sound like Simeon. He said the same thing when he saw the men from Shiloh shadowing us this morning."

Joseph knew it was meant as a joke, but the comment stung all the same. Simeon was an idiot who'd ruined things for all of them and he… he wasn't anything like his half-brother.

Nashu didn't seem to notice either way. "Best thing to do is keep moving, he's only a scout. Besides, the one thing we don't need to do right now is start another war."

That point was enough to make Joseph's grip on his sling slacken a hair, and Nashu nodded in approval. "Keep that handy, but be patient. If they want to fight, I'm sure it'll be obvious." He paused a heartbeat and shot Joseph a pointed look. "You've been practicing?"

Joseph gave a slight nod.

"Good."

Nashu turned to leave, and Joseph hesitated a second, a question caught in his throat, he almost didn't ask, but the words slipped out anyway, "Why did you help them?"

Nashu glanced back, confused, "Help who?"

"Simeon."

For a moment Joseph thought he'd asked too much. Nashu stared at his bow, the muscles in his face tightening as he idly plucked at the string. "Because he was going to do it anyway," Nashu finally answered, "And if we were going to start a war with Hamor, I figured it was best Simeon knew how to win it."

"You could have told Dad though." Even as he said that Joseph couldn't escape a twinge of doubt. Simeon could be… reckless.

Nashu just shook his head. "I try not to be involved in family affairs. Learned that the hard way back in Knossos. I respect your father, Joseph. Wouldn't still be here if I didn't, but… he's not perfect." Nashu shrugged, "I tried to do what I thought would be best. I'm sorry it had to turn out like this."

Joseph didn't know what to say to that, and finally Nashu nodded back towards the traveling column. "Come on, you don't want to get too far separated."

Casting one last glance at the now deserted rocky hilltop, Joseph followed, casually spinning his empty sling into a coil around his lower arm.

The exhausted party that camped that evening in the hills two miles outside Luz was much diminished from the one that had left the gutted city of Shechem two days before. No one had done a hard count on how many of their new slaves had escaped to Shiloh, but Joseph could guess it was at least half, if not more.

In a way though, he was… glad.

It was easier, not having to see their faces, the constant reminders of what had happened. Things were already bad enough. Leaving his small flock of sheep, he trudged with heavy steps through the mingled crowd of talking people and lowing cattle. Only to grind to a halt as a rogue goat barreled by barely a pace in front of him, closely followed by a servant boy.

When he looked up again, the first camel he saw was Leah, closely trailed by Dinah, while Amaleigh and Myrrha walked along not far behind. He looked away and tried to ignore the sudden tightness in his chest. Reminders.

When he finally did find his mom, her camel seemed to have knelt down on its own accord, as if sensing the journey was over and being thoroughly finished with the whole affair. Helping Mom haul herself off the humped beast, it was clear to Joseph that they were all too exhausted to worry about putting up tents. Too exhausted to worry about the men of Luz murdering them in the night.

Amid the tufts of grass, it was the work of only a few minutes to lay out two beds, and as the light went down in the west, Joseph slept. Deep– no dreams, no reminders.

Chapter 15
The House of El

The next morning Joseph stared at the loose piled rock cairn, nervously rubbing his fingers even as a lump like granite settled in his chest. Was *this* it?

After coming all this way, he'd been hoping for something more. Something *real*. Something that might help.

His dad called it *Beth-el*, after all. The House of God. But… this was a pile of rocks. There was no haven, no doorway to somewhere safe. They were camped on a low rocky hill, the dawn shadows casting long arcs across the sea of verdant green turf. All around, their herds spread out along the base of the hill, munching their way through the fresh, ankle-deep grass. A mile's walk to the west the city of Luz sat like a squat stone sentinel on a nearby rise.

When they'd left Shechem, he'd thought his dad was right and his brothers were just being obstinate. Of course they couldn't have held out there and fought off a siege, but now here they were – tired, exposed, no walls to fall back on. They'd lost dozens of servants on the trip down. They didn't even know the terrain. They were in easy striking distance of Luz… and they were counting on a pile of rocks to save them.

Several of his brothers were slowly trickling over to the marker. Finally, Judah spoke up, his voice grim and sarcastic. "Well, we're dead. Anybody up for food?"

The mention of food brought a hungry pang to Joseph's stomach, but he knew Judah well enough to know the invitation didn't include him. Normally Dan and Naphtali might have invited him over, but he'd pretty much trashed that bridge by slugging Naphtali in the face, so…

Joseph sighed, swallowing back the cold rejection. Whatever, maybe he preferred it this way too. His brothers weren't exactly paragons of manners or refinement. He'd get something on his own later and eat it like a civilized person.

Before Judah could get together a group to leave though, Father walked up behind them, noticeably less grim than yesterday. "Excellent," he even had a smile on his face, "you're here."

They weren't *all* there. But with eleven of them that was rare. The six they currently had was close enough to count. Judah turned to look at him, the sarcasm in his voice fading to worry. "Dad, is this it?"

"No," Jacob said bluntly. It was just one word, but Joseph let out a relieved breath he hadn't noticed he was holding. So long as they had a plan besides stare at the rocks and hope for the best.

"If we intend to ask for God's help, we'll need a proper altar. If we're going to do this, we do it as a family." He looked around the small circle. Different faces, different mothers, rivalries, fights, friends all twisted up together in that one word – family.

"That means all of us," Jacob said. "Together."

He shot them a warning look. Whatever problems they had, they could put them aside for one day. "I'd like each of you to bring a stone for an altar. Something decent sized." He held his hands a foot length apart to show. "I'll find one of my own to make it twelve. Later today we'll offer a sacrifice. Understood?"

He waited until he'd gotten nods from all around the circle before continuing. "Excellent. And I'd appreciate it if someone passed that along to all those not here."

He made to leave, but Judah had one other question. "What about the men from Luz? If they come out to fight, what are–"

"They won't," Jacob said in a quiet, confident tone.

"But if they–"

"*They won't*," Jacob reiterated, slow, deliberate. Not angry though, just calm, almost scarily so. "Judah, we're right where we're supposed to be, and the people from Luz won't be fighting, at least not today. Go find your rock." He hesitated a heartbeat and no one moved. "That goes for the rest of you too." He gestured for them to leave, and in a moment they'd scattered like leaves in the breeze.

Joseph waited until the rest of his brothers were gone before walking up next to his dad, who was surveying the low grassy hills surrounding their new camp. "You'll need to get a stone too, Joseph," he said without turning to see who it was.

"I will." Joseph paused, almost afraid to ask the question Judah hadn't thought to pose. "What makes you so sure?"

His dad finally turned to face him. "Sure about what?"

"Luz," Joseph nodded towards the city, "that they won't come out and fight?"

A part of Joseph wondered if his dad was suddenly so confident because he'd gotten another impossible answer, like the voice out of the storm. He was more than a little surprised when his dad grinned, "Nashu." Joseph's face must have made his question obvious because Dad kept on explaining. "An old friend of his lives near Luz. He dropped by earlier to see what we were up too. According to him, everyone's afraid, Luz, Jebus, Shiloh. They all knew Hamor was no mean warrior. They seem to be under the impression that we crushed him in the open field, and now we're heading south to pick another fight. Apparently, no one wants to be on the receiving end. That would also explain why no one from Shiloh came out to fight, even when they could have taken us."

"But," Joseph's mind flashed back to all the servants from Shechem who'd fled into Shiloh the prior day. "Won't everyone who escaped tell them what really happened?"

"Probably, but God has been looking out for us thus far. It will take a couple of days for that news to spread, and a couple more to gather a force. We have time. Hopefully enough."

A few days, Joseph thought. Not really enough to get very far, certainly not south to Grandfather, not with everyone exhausted as they were. He cast one last glance at his dad. He still didn't understand the plan, but his father looked strangely confident, and for an instant he stole a bit of that confidence for himself. Enough to trust that Dad knew what he was doing. Enough to hold back the fear from earlier. Enough to offer a small, "Okay" and turn to go find his rock for their new altar.

***

Joseph suspected his mom would have told him that the stone he chose said something about himself. Large, with sharp angular edges, it looked almost freshly cut, the exact opposite of a worn river stone. He hadn't picked it because it matched his personality though, just trying to be practical. Smooth stones wouldn't fit together well, and the rock was right on the edge of what he could lift. He'd had to take two breaks lugging it back, but he wasn't about to be teased for bringing back a 'pebble'. Dad had asked for rocks, and he wasn't going to give his brothers the satisfaction of bringing back the smallest.

Stumbling back over to the rock cairn, Joseph let the stone fall with a grunt, and a muffled *thwump* on the grass. He wasn't the first one back. Dad was already there. A scattered collection of different stones lay at his feet, mostly chunks of white limestone although there were two rocks stained a dark red.

He still didn't think his choice of stone said anything about him. Even so, his eyes wandered the collection, silently guessing who had brought what. His dad was sitting on one even bigger than Joseph's that he'd no doubt retrieved. The two red ones, unique and stacked off on their own were probably Dan and Naphtali. Four other stones were piled up together, likely Leah's side of the family. Three were decently sized stones and one suspiciously small. It fairly screamed, *I don't care, this is stupid*. Simeon's contribution.

Still catching his breath and trying to ignore the heat of the morning sun, Joseph looked back to see Asher coming up the hill not far behind with a medium sized rock. Joseph's half-brother gave a nod and a curt, 'Hey' as he dropped his stone on the grass. "So, what now?"

Without everyone else back, there wasn't much to do for the moment besides get some food. Joseph wandered back to the pad of grass where he'd spent the night and found his mom busily overseeing two maid servants as they dug holes in the rocky ground for tent poles. She turned to greet him with an unusually buoyant smile, one hand on her baby-bump like she had to keep herself from tipping forward. "Morning, Joseph."

Joseph eyed her an instant, not sure what had her so happy before offering a cautious, "Hi, mom."

His gaze swept over to Remmi and Fannah who'd somehow managed to land the unenviable job of tent-builders. Normally they were a bit more on the ball about avoiding those kinds of tasks, especially given all the other hands in camp. "What's going on?"

"Just putting up somewhere to sleep," his mom said with a cheerful ring to her voice. "If we're going to be here, I might as well be prepared."

"Prepared for…?"

"Well, the baby's coming soon," she said, patting at her bump. She froze, one hand on her belly, like she was feeling something.

"Mom?" Joseph hesitated a second. "Is everything–"

She abruptly relaxed, letting out a relieved puff, and looked back to him. "It's fine," she beamed. "Your little brother's kicking again. I don't think I'll put up the full tent, just enough for some shade and privacy."

She glanced around the little plot she'd selected with a contented sigh. "What about you, Joseph?" she looked up the hill to where Dad was still sitting on his rock. "Your father has you...?

"We're building an altar. I think we're going to sacrifice later."

"Really?" His mom glanced over at Remmi and Fannah. "Hear that, girls? Maybe you should take a break, get some food and clean up for later."

Fannah hesitated a heartbeat, but Remmi didn't need to be told twice. Faster than a flash of lightning, she was brushing the soil off her hands and stood to go with a dipping curtsey and a *yes ma'am*, Fannah two paces behind.

"Are you hungry, Joseph?"

He was starving actually, he hadn't eaten all morning, and soon enough they'd broken out the food. By this point, the bread was four days old and crusty hard, the sort he had to chew on for a while to soften up. His mom was busy snacking on strips of salted mutton, of all things. Not exactly a normal morning food, but glancing over at the half-built tent, there was a bigger problem on Joseph's mind.

"Mom," he finally said, "you know we're not staying?"

"It's just for a week or two," she shrugged. "Until the baby comes."

Joseph paused, "Mom, there's no water."

He hated the way the words cast a shadow over her face. He'd heard plenty of her own adventures from when she'd been younger and watched over grandpa's sheep, so she knew exactly what that meant. If there was nothing to drink, they'd have to move the herds soon or watch the animals start dropping from thirst. There wasn't a choice.

"What about that pond down at the base of the hill?"

Joseph swallowed hard and shook his head. While hunting around for his rock, he'd found there were actually two ponds, a medium one nearby and another little one the next draw over. Neither helped much though.

"It's not spring fed, it's just run-off from the storm and it's not very deep." He'd waded it earlier to check. Dad's rule of thumb was that a day's water for all the herds was ankle deep, twenty paces by twenty paces or knee deep ten paces by ten. Either way, it wasn't that hard to work out.

"If it doesn't rain again, we've got four days… maybe five."

His mom's lips drew tight at that news, and Joseph suddenly wished he could take it back, not tell her. It wasn't her fault that Simeon and Levi had picked the worst possible time to trash everyone's collective lives with their foolishness. They could have waited a couple extra weeks before getting them driven out of their own home. Besides, her knowing didn't change anything, and he… he liked Mom when she was happy.

She nodded anyway, putting on a smile that was transparently fake. "Well, I'm sure it will work out one way or another. Maybe we'll get more rain. Besides, your little brother is due any day now, so I'll see if Althea knows any tricks to make him come sooner."

She sighed and for a few long moments the conversation slipped into an awkward silence. Joseph slowly chewed at bites of tough bread as he tried to think of something… anything else to talk about.

Finally though a question popped to mind. "Hey, I was wondering, you remember those little statues you had me give Dad?"

"What about them?"

"He said that when we left Harran and Grandpa Laban came after us, he went through the camp looking for them. How did you hide them? Dad said he didn't know."

At the question an elfin, almost girlish grin tugged at his mom's face. It reminded him of Myrrha, back when she'd been ten and fighting not to blurt out a secret.

For a few heartbeats he watched his mom's expression bounce between a flicker of uncertainty and trying not to laugh.

"I suppose you're old enough to know," she finally said, nodding to herself. "So, it's important to understand, I had them down in my saddle. Your grandfather was furious… to put it mildly. Your father was upset too. That wasn't helping things. He told your grandfather," she paused an instant like she was trying to remember the exact words. "If you find your gods with anyone here, he will not live…" Her voice trailed off, a look on her face like the memory was strangely fresh. "So, not the best start to things…"

Chapter 16
Memories

There were some things that you couldn't *un*-hear.

Like how his mom had avoided getting caught with grandfather's idols. Yeah, he would have been perfectly fine not knowing about her secrets, ever.

Unfortunately, he was stuck with that now.

As Joseph traipsed back over to admire his father's new rock collection, he found Dad quietly rolling the bulky stone he'd been seated on across the grass.

"Joseph," his dad gestured him over. "Can you put your stone – about here." Jacob pointed to a spot on the turf right next to his own.

Joseph did, straining to lift the rock and suddenly wondering how he'd managed to tote it all the way up the hill earlier.

As he set it down and stepped back, his father gave him a short nod. "Thank you, son."

Joseph waited a long moment for his father to tell him what else to do. Dad didn't.

Joseph finally asked, "Did you need me to move something?"

"It's fine." His father grunted a little as he gave another hefty push to move his own large stone. "This is something I need to do myself. Close the circle, so to speak."

Joseph nodded but didn't really have a clue what that cryptic sentence meant. It took him a minute to play out the words in his head. "Dad," he asked, "what happened here? Why is it so special?"

It was enough for his father to pause, wordless, eying him for an instant. Finally, his dad inhaled a long breath and went back to work. Joseph was certain he wasn't going to say anymore, right up until his dad started talking.

"I stole something from my brother, your Uncle Esau. Something I couldn't give back. I was impatient, and foolish and I…"

His voice trailed off as he turned to meet Joseph's gaze. For maybe the only time Joseph could remember, he caught something like a misty cloud in his dad's eyes, a sort of awful regret, enough to make Joseph swallow. "I broke things between us, and I came *here* trying to get away from it all."

"Broke how?" Joseph was almost scared to ask, "What did you take?"

His father sighed and spoke the word as barely a whisper.

"Everything."

***

Thirty Years Earlier

Jacob pressed on through the rock-strewn grass, even as the last rays of day faded behind the western hills. To his left, Luz was backlit by the dying light, threads of blue-grey smoke lacing the sky like a tapestry.

He needed somewhere to sleep, but glancing over at the city, he knew he wouldn't find a place there. The gates would have closed at sundown, and even if they hadn't… well, most places weren't that friendly to outsiders who staggered into town smelling of a journey and without much silver to spend.

He *did* need to stop though, if only so he didn't turn an ankle trying to walk in the dark. The image briefly flashed through his head, him limping back into camp

123

like an idiot. Soon to be a *dead* idiot, he mused grimly, at least if Esau had anything to say about it.

The thought brought with it a surge of regret that Jacob had to fight to force back down. He'd made the right decision, he repeated for about the hundredth time. Esau didn't deserve Father's blessing. He'd never cared. Besides, it was his mother's idea and–

And yet, Jacob still felt a churn in his stomach over what he'd done.

Well, he sighed, if it was wrong he was paying the price well enough. Life had turned to absolute *kabû* ever since. Father was furious, Esau was, *literally,* plotting to murder him, and now here he was – alone – running – exiled off to Haran, hoping to find an uncle he'd never met.

Yeah, life was fantastic, and… he missed Mom.

It was darker now, and he'd been walking since morning. As the weariness sank into his muscles, he finally came to a halt, his legs feeling strange to not be moving. It was too late to build much of a fire, and this close to town he doubted anything would bother him. The lions and bears would be up in the hills, away from the people. They were out looking for lambs, not someone who would put up a fight.

Finding a place to lay down was really just an exercise in choosing the least miserable spot. Even exhausted as he was, Jacob rolled around more than a few times, using his cloak as a blanket against the nighttime chill. Eventually, he found a patch of softer grass and a small rock to lay on so he wouldn't be walking all day tomorrow with a crick in his neck.

Closing his eyes, Jacob tried not to think of everything wrong with the world, tried not to see himself standing on the edge of the land where he'd spent most of his life, utterly alone. He let the sounds of the night fill his head. The hum of locusts, the far-off bleats of goats towards the city, and the gentle whisp of grass in the breeze until… that faded too.

***

Jacob's eyes flashed open, confronted by a sudden brightness in the night. Sitting up, his eyes were drawn to a tall man striding across the grass towards him. For some reason, the first thought that came to mind was that his face was clean shaven, like an Egyptian.

Except he was no Egyptian.

Draped in a spotless white tunic cut on an angle at his knees, the man had his hair trimmed short and wore a belt that gleamed of golden bronze.

Jacob pulled in a nervous breath as the man came close, but he passed by, hurrying about his business, with only a curt nod of acknowledgement.

Jacob's head turned to follow the strange man, and when it did, Jacob froze, his eyes straining to take in the sight behind him.

It was like he'd been standing at the gates of Akkad itself and only just now noticed. Behind him stretched a wide stone stairway soaring like a mountain into the sky. At its summit the stairway vanished into a cloud that had split open, pouring out a light like the sun across the darkened landscape. Each step glowed with beautiful carvings inlaid with wrought silver that shimmered like it was still molten. At the foot of the mighty stairway stood two more men, sentinels, both clothed in white with bronze armor that glowed like stars, and impressively long, two-handed swords buckled around their waists.

Jacob saw they didn't try to stop the man who'd just passed him. Instead, one guard smiled and stepped aside as the man in white alighted the stairs and started the long hike to the top.

Gazing at the steps into the heavens, Jacob stood, watching more men ascending and descending, dozens, all in the same flawless white. Out of the corner of his eye, he caught another gleam of silver, and his head slowly turned to see three more men. They all stood not five paces away, utterly at ease, like they'd always been there, just waiting for him to notice. They had more swords belted around their waists, each worked to a length no smith could match. Even as Jacob stared, one raised a hand with a polite, almost amused grin, that he somehow understood as a farewell. The question flashed in his mind, had they been… following him?

Before he could ask, the man moved toward the steps, gesturing the other two after him.

As the first three men departed on the long trek skyward, another group of warriors, seven of them, were reaching the bottom of the stairs. Coming close, the leader met Jacob's gaze and drew his sword with a blade like golden fire in salute. While Jacob was still staring in amazement, the soldier took a place at his side. A confused Jacob glanced back to see the remainder of the strange warriors arraying themselves in a loose cordon around him. Before he could wonder at what they were doing though, the first warrior caught his gaze, gesturing towards the summit of the towering stairs.

Then, to Jacob's absolute shock, the warrior reversed his exquisite blade. The point sank deep into the soft earth, and the man dropped onto one knee, bowing before the stairway to heaven.

Jacob looked to the dizzying top, still shrouded in cloud. From within he caught a gathering glow, rising like the sun at dawn. He tried to watch, but at last Jacob had to look away. When he did, a radiance enough to burn the world flashed out from the cloud. He couldn't look at the light that shone like a sky full of suns, but Jacob caught a glimpse of the man beside him. For the one instant he could bear to watch, Jacob saw the man as he truly was. A face that glowed with power and silver-pale clothes that lit up in the dazzling blaze, richer and more vibrant, like every color rolled into one beautiful tunic.

From above came a Voice that cut the air like a peal of thunder and sent Jacob to his knees. "I am the Lord, the God of Abraham your father and the God of Isaac. The land on which you lie I will give to you and to your offspring."

"Your offspring shall be like the dust of the earth, and you shall spread abroad to the west and to the east and to the north and to the south, and in you and your offspring shall all the families of the earth be blessed."

"Behold, I am with you and will keep you wherever you go, and will bring you back to this land. For I will not leave you until I have done what I have promised you."

The Voice finished, and even with his eyes pressed tight shut and his face towards the ground, Jacob could see the starburst that washed out around him like he was staring into the sun until…

Jacob bolted upright drawing in a sharp breath as his eyes frantically blinked against the glare that had been there only a second before.

Except it was gone.

It took a few heartbeats to see it was still night. The stars shone overhead, and the moon had vanished beyond the horizon. On a far hill, even the city of Luz had grown dark.

It was just him. Just a dream.

Or… maybe not.

Casting a last look at the place where the stairway had been, Jacob could swear he caught a glimpse of a fading halo. Like the last glimmer of a world beyond his sight before it pulled back behind the veil.

An awful terror stabbed at his chest. It wasn't *just* a dream, and he'd been sleeping at…

Even in the dark, Jacob bowed his head, and took a long breath. "Forgive me," he whispered, hoping God would understand. "Surely the Lord is in this place, and I did not know it."

He wasn't sure how long he sat there, head bowed. When he finally dared to open his eyes, he felt some of the dread ease away, replaced by the words from the dream. "Behold, I am with you."

Looking at the spot where the stairway had stood, Jacob couldn't escape a lingering awe at everything he'd just witnessed. For a moment his mind wandered back through the scene, committing it to memory. The gleaming stairs, the warriors that had surrounded him, the Voice from heaven. Someone he didn't understand had just promised him the whole land he'd walked today and more and… he didn't want to forget.

For a long time he didn't move, and overhead the silver moon rose towards the summit of the sky. Finally, not sure what else to say, he summed it all up with the simple words, "What an awesome place this is. This is none other than the house of God. This is the gate of heaven."

***

"So, what did you do?" Joseph asked eagerly.

"Well… eventually I went back to sleep," his dad said with a dry humor, even as he placed a final stone on the altar. "I was tired, and it was–" he had to think for a second, "probably another week and a half to Harran."

Joseph waited a second for him to continue, more serious.

"The next morning, I set up that." He pointed to the small cairn a dozen paces away, "The top rock was the one I used to sleep on. I poured a little oil on it, and named it Bethel, for it was the House of God. Then I left, and I haven't been back since."

Something about all that struck Joseph, like a stone falling perfectly into place. "Is that what you meant?"

128

he suddenly burst out. "Last week, before we met with Hamor, you said something about finishing the journey. Is this what you were talking about?"

His dad eyed him a moment, an impressed smile tugging at his lips. "It is."

"Then why didn't we?" Joseph asked, suddenly confused. "If God is… like you said, why haven't we ever…?"

His dad let out a heavy sigh. "I was going to." He took a careful seat on the grass and Joseph found a spot beside him. "Come back, that is." Dad pursed his lips for a moment, and when he continued his voice was halting, like he wasn't entirely sure he should say more. "What you saw a few days ago, Joseph, that – wasn't the first time God told me to come back here."

"Before we left your grandfather Laban in Harran, God appeared and told me to return here. At the time things were… difficult between Laban and I, so we came back…" His voice trailed off as though that were somehow the end of it.

"But not all the way?" Joseph still couldn't understand.

"Not all the way," his father agreed. Joseph had to bite at his tongue to hold back the 'why' poised to come out. He'd never seen his dad like this. It was almost like he was scared.

For a while his dad was silent, but finally he twisted around to look behind, like he wanted to make sure they were alone. "There was one other thing that happened here," he said. "After I set up the marker, I – made a promise. I told God that if He would be with me and would watch over me on the journey I was taking and would give me food to eat and clothes to wear so that I return safely to my father's household, then the Lord would be my God and the stone that I had set up as a pillar would be God's house, and of all that He gave me I would give Him a tenth."

Joseph frowned, "Well, that's not so bad."

"Isn't it?" His father arched his eyebrows in a skeptical look. "God promised me this whole land we're sitting in and descendants without number, and I promised him a tenth of what he gave. The land, I suppose is a small thing, but..."

He nodded at Joseph and suddenly it clicked exactly what his dad meant. A chill raced down Joseph's spine. "Us," he whispered with a gulp.

His dad gave a second dour nod. "You see why I wasn't so eager to be here." He sighed, "I'm not really sure what God will ask of me. Maybe nothing, maybe something I *can* give... maybe something I *can't*."

He shot Joseph a side glance. "When you're older I'll tell you what He asked of my grandfather Abraham. It's enough to make one cautious."

"Anyway," Jacob took a long breath like he was nerving himself, "I've been staying away a very long time, but it seems God won't wait forever."

Joseph nodded, suddenly more than a little scared himself. He glanced up at the cloudless sky, the trepidation of what came next gnawing at him, and a thought struck him. "You said God was up there?" he pointed skyward, "In the dream."

"Well, it looked a little different," Jacob mused. "But yes. Why?"

"Well, if He's up there, I assume He can see us. Why bring us all this way when He could just... tell you whatever He was going to say?"

The question was enough to give his dad pause "I don't know." He shrugged, "I suppose He's giving us the courtesy of waiting until we're ready." His dad glanced up at the sun, which was at about midmorning. "Speaking of which," Jacob finally pushed himself upright off his spot in the grass and rose to his feet with a slight pop from his good leg. "I suppose, one way or another, we're about ready." He looked down at Joseph. "Would you tell your mother we're going to make an offering? I'll let Leah and the others know."

Joseph nodded as his dad made to leave, his last words hanging in the air. "We'll see soon enough why God has called us here."

Chapter 17
El-Shaddai

Standing beside his mother and brothers, wearing his best tunic, Joseph tried to ignore the awful twisting like leverets playing in his stomach. A dozen steps away his dad gently lowered his torch to the bundles of fresh kindling stacked around the altar.

The torch flames licked at the wood, refusing to catch.

Until they did.

His dad tossed the torch in among the kindling and stepped back as the fire took the dry wood. For a moment Joseph stared at the leaping flames. So, this was it, the thought raced through his mind, the end of the waiting, a storm set in motion and rolling inexorably closer. God was coming.

The hungry fire blossomed and licked at their offering, sizzling and popping as it seared the fresh cut lamb and the small pile of ground flour laid on the stones. A slight wind to his back pushed the smoke away, and carried on the breeze, he could catch the little noises of a hundred and fifty slaves, servants, and followers arrayed on the hillside behind him.

Everyone. Waiting.

Forcing his fingers to stop rapping together, Joseph glanced at his brothers. At least *they* weren't worried. Next to him, Judah was at ease, here because Dad wanted it, nothing more. A dutiful son.

Then again, Judah hadn't seen, had he?

He hadn't heard the Voice in the storm, he didn't know about the stairway to the sky. He wasn't expecting God… and he didn't know what Dad had promised.

Scuffing a foot in the grass, Joseph's eyes cast back towards the flames as they bloomed higher, the fire catching in full force, and the smoke tracing swirls as it drifted skyward.

A half dozen paces in front of them, his father knelt down on both knees and sat back on his heels. For a heartbeat Joseph wasn't certain if they were meant to follow, until he caught a trace of motion out of the corner of his eye.

His mom and Leah both knelt.

So, yes.

Dropping down, Joseph heard the distinctive swish of skirts and tunics as the crowd behind followed suit. In the silent stillness that followed, time seemed to stretch on forever. Smoke rose, the bundles of wood popped in the heat, and Joseph had to fight to keep his mind from wandering. A dozen tiny details seemed to try and muscle their way in. Things he usually never would have noticed. At his feet the grass clumped in low patches on the ground that fanned out like a field of little green bushes. Further back, he caught the faint lowing of cattle from the base of the hill. His knees were starting to hurt as they pressed on the hard dirt, the sun was hot on his back and he felt a bead of sweat tracing its way down his neck.

Kneeling in the late morning heat, a part of him was starting to wonder if anything would happen. Maybe this wasn't what his dad thought at all. Maybe God wasn't coming.

From behind a sudden breeze plastered his tunic against his back, bringing a welcome cool with it. Glancing back to the fire Joseph blinked. The smoke was… dancing?

The fire was a stage on which the smoke from their sacrifice twirled an intricate geometric ballet. The wind caught grey twirls and spirals in a precise vortex that twisted higher, morphing as it went.

Joseph's eyes followed the beautiful weave skywards, where he caught a glint like the sun on glass. A flash of light far off in the cloudless blue expanse. Confused, he watched as the glimmer of light seemed to take form, twisting a moment in an elaborate dance then abruptly wrapping into itself until it was only a single point.

Then the gleaming core blasted outwards. A translucent shock raced across the sky sweeping towards the horizon in every direction and condensing a trail of clouds in its wake.

In an instant the sky was transformed from bright and blue, to a flat ceiling of slate grey. Joseph stared, lost, but then his gaze was drawn back towards the light.

He could swear it shone brighter now beneath the grey veil. It hovered there, like a pinhole punched in the sky. Everywhere around him, he could hear a low hum, a noise like the gentle buzz of cicadas in the evening, the kind that you only noticed when you listened for it. But it was there, growing more clear, more distinct, until an abrupt thunderclap split the air. Even kneeling, Joseph nearly jumped in shock, as overhead the sky tore open.

A pillar of gentle light stabbed down around their altar, and in the instant of stillness that followed, Joseph caught the drifting notes of music overhead. Even faint and faraway it was the sort of melody he could have listened to forever, an intricate, buoyant tune that brought a smile to his face just hearing it.

In camp, their music was mostly singing, accompanied by timbrels, drums, and the occasional flute. But the song above was sublime, they might as well have been scratching patterns in the dirt to try and compare. Music distilled down to its essence, without any cracking voices, missed notes or off-tone accompaniment. Sounds he'd never heard before, all woven together into a vast tapestry of song.

His mind was still trying to wrap itself around the floating anthem, when a light like a thousand suns blossomed overhead. Joseph had to shield his eyes as something impossibly bright descended in the pillar of light around the altar. The radiant star touched at the ground a pace in front of his dad, sending a tremor rippling through the earth beneath his feet.

Joseph gulped, eyes pressed tight shut, as a hurricane of questions filled his head. What was happening? Was God here to rescue them from the Canaanites, or collect on his dad's promise? Or something else entirely? And why them? Why here? The melody above still hung like gold in the air, but amid it all, Joseph wasn't sure if he should be awed or terrified.

Then the light spoke, a single word in a Voice strong but gentle that swept over Joseph, bringing a tremendous calm. It left all his anxious questions discarded like fallen twigs, unimportant.

Suddenly he wasn't afraid.

"Jacob," the Voice declared.

Joseph was barely close enough to hear his dad's whispered reply. "Yes, God."

For an instant that dragged into eternity the Voice was silent, before finally it continued, louder… bigger than before. "Your name is Jacob, but you will no longer be called Jacob; your name will be Israel."

The Voice rose to a thunder as it continued, "I am El-Shaddai; be fruitful and increase in number. A nation and a community of nations will come from you, and kings will be among your descendants. The land I gave to Abraham and Isaac I also give to you, and I will give this land to your descendants after you."

For a long moment the words hung in the air, like
the whole world was singing at hearing the Voice. Then
a brilliance flashed out, and even face to the ground,
eyes closed, Joseph could still see the ocean of light
that washed around them.

Chapter 18
Deborah

Joseph was still trying to piece together everything he'd just witnessed. Even as he helped his mom back down the hillside to her tent, the memories circled like falcons in his head – the remembrance of the Voice, the words of God etched in his mind.

And after… when the Beacon that washed them in a river of light had ascended, and the song to make him weep for its beauty had faded. When they'd dared to look up and found rays of sun cutting through the fading clouds. When his dad had looked back across the stunned crowd. "Is anyone still afraid?"

After what they'd just seen, it felt almost silly. They'd just watched God descend like a star from a gateway in the sky and promise them a future bigger than he could have imagined.

Joseph glanced from the hill towards the squat walled city of Luz in the distance. This morning the city had looked like doom, a foreboding sentinel waiting to strike them all down. Now, Joseph wasn't sure he could be scared of it if he wanted to.

Then there was the other bit. He'd promised the captives from Shechem their freedom.

"Those of you from Shechem," his dad called across the silent hillside. "We have done you a great evil, and there is nothing I can do to recompense you. I cannot replace what you have lost, but those of you who wish to leave and return to what relatives you still have, are free to go. We will provide you what we can. Any who wish to stay will be treated fairly, and free to live among us. It does not set things right, but it is what we have to give."

Joseph shook his head, a chill running down his spine at the memory of his dad's voice, somber, remorseful, but hard as flint. At any other moment freeing half the slaves with a pronouncement like that would have set off a riot.

Except today.

Today, when he'd knelt before God.

Eyes had gone wide, he'd heard Simeon breathe in a sharp hiss, and Reuben had winced like he'd stepped on a sewing needle. All of them shocked at watching so much of their inheritance evaporate in a few simple words. But no one had dared object, not after what they'd beheld.

In truth, Joseph admired his dad for having the courage to do it. No one agreed. The argument was written on every face, but he'd done it anyway and… it was better like this. After so much death and violence and fear and hurt. It was better like this.

Next to him, Mom smiled as they waded through the ankle-deep grass. "That was a lovely song. Don't you think, Joseph?"

"Yeah," he nodded with a grin of his own, "it was like listening to–"

His voice abruptly cut off as a woman's pained gasp tore the air. Joseph looked over, and his throat went ash dry when he saw who was kneeling on the grass, clutching at her chest. "Dede!"

He wasn't the first to reach her. Issachar dashed over and dropped down beside Dede, a frantic look on his face like he didn't know what to do. He scooted aside as Dad reached them a moment later and Joseph darted up a few heartbeats behind. "Deborah," Dad asked, frantic. "What is it?"

His grandmother drew in a hissing breath, her face screwed up in pain, "I…" She winced, and didn't finish.

His dad looked up, desperate, "Samas!" he shouted for the doctor. "Samas, get over here!"

***

Half an hour later, Joseph aimed yet another kick at the same clump of grass he'd been gradually tearing out of the ground each time he paced by. Inside Jacob's tent he could hear voices, Dad, his mom, Leah, Samas. He couldn't make out all the words, but from the quiet tears he'd heard earlier, it didn't sound good.

A few feet away Zebulun and Issachar were both sitting near the tent, listening. Judah, Dan and Naphtali were busy in quiet conversation a little way off, while the rest of his brothers were seated in a small circle, no one quite sure what to do. Dinah and a few of the other girls had found a spot under a tree nearby. Apparently, they all felt like they needed to be here.

"Joseph," Zebulun shot him a glare, his voice a curt whisper, "Can you go pace somewhere else?"

Joseph didn't dignify him with a response. Instead, he just crossed his arms and gave the tuft of grass one more scuff with his sandal.

Pacing twice more in front of his dad's tent, he looked back at hearing the whisk of the tent flap being pulled aside. Samas and Dad both stepped out, conversing in hushed whispers, and were instantly swept up in a flurry of questions.

"Dad, what's happening?"

"Why can't we see her?"

"Is Dede going to be…"

Dad raised a hand to cut them all off, "Deborah is…" his voice trailed off. "She's… she may not have much longer."

The words hung in the air for a stunned heartbeat and Joseph felt a coldness like ice in his chest. Everything else sort of drifted to the background.

Dede was dying?

Nearby he vaguely heard Issachar speak up, his voice haunted. "What do you mean? She was fine earlier. How can she just…?"

"Issachar, Dede is old," Jacob said. "She was looking after *me* when I was a baby and…" His voice died in his throat, his face blank, a dam fighting to hold back a torrent.

Samas spoke up, "You should probably start saying your goodbyes."

"How long does she have?" Judah asked, ever practical.

Samas shook his head, "It's difficult to tell with these sorts of things. It could be tonight, it could be three days." He paused, "I… would suspect tonight though. If you could, go in one or two at a time, the one thing she doesn't need right now is more excitement." He waited until they'd all nodded before stepping aside from the tent flap.

There was a moments discussion who would go in first, but Joseph was still trying to catch up. "Samas," he caught the man's arm, desperation creeping into his voice, "there has to be something you can do? Right?"

The middle-aged doctor sighed. "Joseph, if she was sick or injured maybe, but… I don't have something to fix old age." He shook his head. "Maybe your father's God could, but…"

Joseph understood, but amid the panic of losing Dede he didn't care. "Please, there has to be something."

Samas's expression seeming to think on it for a moment. "I can make her more comfortable." He met Joseph's eyes. "It won't fix things but…"

Joseph nodded, eager, "What do you need?"

"Just some water and the willow bark powder," Samas said half muttering to himself. "I think Myrrha packed it, so it's probably in Althea's tent."

"I can get it." Joseph nodded, turning to leave.

"You know what it looks like?" Samas asked, surprised.

Joseph vaguely remembered the little clay pot Myrrha had shown him a few days earlier. "I can find it," he said breaking into a jog before Samas could object.

He had more trouble finding Myrrha's tent than he'd expected. He'd gotten so used to *where* it was that he could probably could have walked there in his sleep back… home? It felt strange calling the Ebal Vale home, especially since they'd lived in tents, but… it felt like home, even now, after everything that had happened.

Anyway, now it was a new camp, and all the tents were scrambled up. No more herb garden to mark out Myrrha's. He found it though, the front flap tied open, leaving just a semi-transparent linen curtain to keep out the dust and bugs.

"Myrrha?" Joseph waited a second before stooping and pushing aside the linen to glance inside, she never minded. "Myrrha, are you–"

He froze at the sight of a girl who definitely *wasn't* Myrrha curled up, on a mat in the corner. The girl's eyes fluttered open to see him, and she drew in a sharp breath, "Joseph?"

"Amaleigh?"

Her expression turned cold, "What do you want?"

Joseph hesitated, "I thought this was Myrrha's tent."

"Well, not all of us are special enough to have our own place," Amaleigh snapped, her voice on edge. "There wasn't much room. Myrrha and Althea were nice enough to offer me a spot, even if…" Amaleigh glanced around the strange tent. Althea had thrown away some of her crazy apothecary decor, but she and Myrrha had kept a lot of it. A few sprigs of drying leaves still hung outside, their last little harvest before leaving, and inside… well, suffice to say Amaleigh had been lucky to find any space for a mat at all amid the piled baskets and pots. For a moment Joseph could read the rest of the sentence in Amaleigh's eyes, 'Even if it was cramped and smelled strange.'

She didn't say that though, just sighed with a frown. "If you want Myrrha, she's not here."

"I didn't, actually," Joseph stammered. "I just need some willow bark powder." His eyes drifted across the jumble, and he mumbled a curse at the absurdity of trying to find that little clay pot he remembered amid all this.

Not sure what else to do, Joseph started hurriedly rummaging through the first basket he could find, before quickly deciding the willow bark powder wasn't there.

Amaleigh watched him a moment before quietly asking, "What do you need bark powder for?"

"Medicine," Joseph said, "for Dede."

"Dede? Is that the old lady?"

A part of him bristled at hearing her referred to as an *old lady*, but… Amaleigh didn't know, did she. "Yeah."

"Is she going to be okay?"

Joseph didn't answer, like if he didn't admit what was happening, it wouldn't be real. He just kept searching.

Amaleigh watched for a moment before standing. "What's it look like?"

"It's a little clay pot, squat, fat, with a sawdust sort of powder inside."

Amaleigh went to searching beneath a stack of straw baskets in a corner. She pulled up a few pots, but none that looked right. They worked a minute or two before Joseph felt the silence getting awkward.

"So uhh… I guess you're leaving," he finally said. "Now that you're free and all."

Amaleigh glanced over at him. "Maybe," she said in an unconvincing tone. "I might."

He paused, "Why wouldn't you?" He didn't mean it to come off rude but an instant after the words were out, he realized they were… blunt–*er* than he'd intended.

Amaleigh shrugged, "It's not like I have anywhere to go. My family never had many relatives near Shechem. Supposedly there were some up north towards Damascus, but…"

But that was a long way, especially for a girl her age traveling alone.

"What about Isnah and her mom. You weren't going with them?"

"Isnah's back at Shiloh."

Joseph's voice trailed off, "Oh."

Amaleigh didn't respond and just focused back on rummaging through another basket.

"They *might* take me in," Amaleigh added after a pause. "But that's a long trip too. And I'm not sure what good I'd be when I got there. Just the nobody girl from out of town. Get married off to the boy no one else wants and…"

She shook her head. "Maybe I'll just stay here. Especially after… whatever that was that just happened at your altar."

She shot him a side glance. "How is it… here?"

"You mean normally," Joseph tried to crack a bit of a joke. "When we're not on the run and having… God… happen."

"Yeah."

"It's," he stopped his search to think on his answer for a second, "okay, I guess. Depends, really. It's easier if you're not constantly on Leah's bad side, like me. But, you're tight with Dinah, so you'd probably be fine."

Joseph dropped the lid back down on another basket, and stepped back, fingers tapping in frustration. Where was that stupid pot?

He cast about for a moment before noticing Myrrha's special box, the one with all the glass jars she'd shown him. It was stuck at the bottom of a pile, but it was medicine. Right idea at least.

Hurrying over, he peered around the back and let out a sigh of relief when he saw a squat little clay pot. With the pot stuck right at the back, he had to half slide in behind the pile to even get his hand close.

"You can ask Myrrha about staying," Joseph added, "I'm sure she could give you an opinion."

He hesitated, mentioning Myrrha bring back a rush of other emotions that he wasn't sure what to do with. What *was* Myrrha's opinion. Did she still hate him? He swallowed it back, instead stretching an arm for the pot.

"Maybe you're–" Amaleigh must have looked up, "Joseph, stop!" she half shouted. "You'll knock it all over."

"It's… right…" He stretched for the pot, and just managed to grab the rough clay.

Wiggling his way out, he found Amaleigh nearby with a disapproving frown, holding back the pile from crashing to the dirt.

"Thanks," Joseph nodded. He checked inside the pot and felt a surge of triumph at seeing the coarse grey willow bark powder. "I've got to go."

He hurriedly made for the tent flap, but hesitated as he swept aside the wispy curtain. Glancing back, he saw Amaleigh standing there in the middle of the tent looking… very sad and alone.

For that one instant, about to walk back and say goodbye to Dede with nothing he could really do about it… he kind of understood the hurt written on her face… just a little.

"I'm sorry."

Amaleigh glanced over in surprise but seemed to understand what he meant. She didn't answer except for a tiny nod, swallowing back whatever else might have come out.

He turned to leave, her last words following him out the front of the tent, "I hope she gets better."

The words brought a sinking feeling to Joseph's chest. Yeah, he did too.

Chapter 19
Goodbye

"Dede?" Joseph nervously poked his head into the tent holding a little cup of Samas's mixture. He'd more or less cut in front of everyone to get in, one of the perks of bearing medicine.

The woman who looked back at him from a flaxen mat seemed smaller than he remembered, but her grey hair was still tied up in the same messy bun from earlier. Maybe it was just that she was lying down.

"Joseph?" Dede craned her neck to look at him, still with a smile on her face.

He'd been in such a hurry that he hadn't actually planned anything to say, so he just started with the obvious, "I uh… brought you something." He stepped closer and knelt down to offer her the cup.

Dede sniffed at the cloudy water and wrinkled her nose. "Oh, don't tell me it's more medicine." A flicker of resigned amusement played across her wrinkled features.

"Samas said it would help you feel better."

"Will it now?" she asked, sarcastic. She drew in a raspy breath. "I suppose if it kills me it's not the end of the world."

She gestured for the cup.

Joseph took a moment to help prop her up enough to take a sip. Dede winced a little before her first taste, but after one swallow, her expression brightened considerably and she downed the whole cup in a just a few gulps. "That was… excellent." She settled back on a few cushions. "Sweet, a little earthy."

"He added some honey to help with the taste."

"Huh," she mused, "you should tell him to try that with the rest of his medicine. I swear, sometimes I wonder if that madman hasn't had it out for me this whole time."

It was the sort of joke he'd heard her make a dozen times before, but suddenly Joseph had a hard time mustering a smile. He just looked at the floor and felt Dede's eyes on him. For a long moment neither said anything. Finally, Joseph looked up to see her with a sort of melancholy smile. "It's ok to say it, Joseph."

Was it? A part of him wasn't so sure. Like if he said she was dying, then she really was, and there was nothing he could do, and…

It just sort of slipped out, "I don't want you to go."

For an instant his words hung there between them. Admitting it must have made things real, because the next heartbeat his eyes pressed tight shut as the tears came.

"It's alright, Joseph." He felt Dede's arms pulling him close, her hug surprisingly strong for how frail she looked. "It's okay."

"But it's not," he tried to brush away the tears. "You're…" He couldn't bring himself to say it.

"I'm what? Dying?" Dede gave a long sigh and settled back on her cushions. "It happens you know. At least, that's what I've been told."

That was hardly an encouraging thought, and she must have seen it on his face as she continued. "I know it's hard to understand when you're young, but when you get to be my age, it's not as bad as it seems. You get old enough and everything starts hurting. Just getting up in the morning gets to be a fight. After a while you get tired." She sighed and patted his arm, "I've been fighting for a long time. Someday you'll understand."

Joseph gave a weak nod, but… he didn't really think he would. "Are you feeling better?"

She struggled to pull in another halting breath. "A little bit." Deborah gave a thin smile, "I am sorry I won't get to see the baby. But I did get to see you grow up Joseph, and…" She paused a moment to catch her breath, even talking took an effort. "Now, I guess you'll have to be there instead of me. You be strong, Joseph," Dede said. "For your mom."

Joseph took her hand, cold despite the blankets and nodded, "I will."

That seemed to satisfy Dede, and she exhaled a lingering breath, her eyes sliding shut for a moment and her whole figure seeming to shrink down into her mat. "Good," she murmured. "You know, I was kind of hoping I'd have a few extra weeks. This is all more sudden than I thought."

Joseph frowned, she was making it sound almost like… "You knew this would happen?"

"Ehhh, you get old enough and you start to notice the signs. I had an inkling. Figured it wasn't worth bringing up. It'd just end with Samas getting his claws in me and making it all very miserable. Better to spend the time with everyone." Another pause to catch her breath, "That said, if I had to pick a day to go, this is a pretty good one. I got to see something amazing after all."

For a moment her eyes fixed on him with her intense, 'I'm serious' glare. Suddenly Joseph had a strange feeling, like he was six and about to be sent to bed. "You promise me something, Joseph." Her hand tightened on his, "Promise me you won't forget what happened today, up on that hill."

"I…" that was a strange thing to ask, but he nodded anyway. "Of course not."

"You say that, but you're not old enough to start losing memories." Deborah shook her head. "It's not so much that you forget, you know, just… life keeps happening, all the time. The memories, they get… misplaced, and eventually you forget that they're there at all." She gave a wan grin and caught her breath. "It's easier to do than you think. And what happened up there… you're lucky to see something like that once in a lifetime. Don't lose it, Joseph."

Dede slid back into her cushion, like the talk had taken a lot out of her.

Honestly, Joseph still didn't really understand. He wasn't sure how he could have forgotten seeing God show up ten paces in front of him, even if he'd wanted to. Dede seemed very insistent though, and it was a small thing. Wandering back through the memory of the voice up on the hill, Joseph fixed it in his mind. The mental equivalent of when Myrrha would have him stand back and hold up a tunic to look over after stitching in a patch. Just making sure she hadn't forgotten any of the important bits before setting it aside.

"I won't forget," he whispered. "I promise."

"Good." Her eyes were closed now, but Dede gave his hand one final squeeze.

He waited there a minute, not wanting to leave until Samas poked his head inside. "Joseph," he gestured him towards the exit, "it's time."

Right. Joseph sighed and swallowed back the lump in his throat. Time, it was all run out, wasn't it. He blinked back a mist in his eyes, then stooped, pull aside the tent flap and looked back, wishing he could drag the moment out into forever. "Goodbye."

Chapter 20
Lost Dreams

Joseph plodded along, his feet heavy on the road. Thankfully the sheep weren't making much of a fuss, they were just as ready as him for this trip to be over.

"Come on." He flicked a stick at the hindmost ewe, trying to speed along the herd as best he could. Not that it really mattered. They were moving at the pace of the slowest group, which was probably Gad and Zebulun towards the back with the goats. But he still felt the urgency inside like a sundial shadow sliding towards evening.

They needed to hurry, just… no one else seemed to care.

***

Two Days Earlier

Dede would have liked the place where they buried her, Joseph hoped. An ancient looking oak tree, with a trunk so wide he could barely wrap his arms halfway around. They'd dug her a grave at the base between two roots, each as thick as his arm. Up above, the trunk was scarred with stubs of branches where boughs had snapped off in storms over the years. It still boasted a leafy green canopy near the top though, enough to cast a shadow of filtered light at the base. And behind all the broken limbs there were new shoots sprouting out as well. Battered but alive. She would have been happy.

For a while after they'd finished, Joseph stood by the grave as everyone started to trickle away. Eventually it was just him and Issachar left.

Issachar had always been close with Dede too. In a family where pettiness seemed the rule so much of the time, she'd been one of the few people who didn't get caught up in the nasty little game. For Joseph, it was being the odd man out. For Issachar, it was being fifth brother out of six, not the baby, but still small enough to get picked on. Miserable either way, he supposed.

He'd been hoping everyone would clear out so he could just have some time alone. Idly scraping his sandal in the grass, Joseph glanced over to see Issachar watching him too. Neither said a word, but Joseph got the message. Issachar wanted some time alone with Dede also. One of those things neither could really ask for.

Joseph sighed. Well, he could come back this evening. It would probably be cooler then anyway.

Turning, he wandered back towards the jumbled camp they'd erected. He wasn't really going anywhere in particular as he walked through the unfamiliar sprawl of tents. Mostly his brain kept noting how everyone was camped in the wrong place. The city he'd gotten so used to was all scrambled up.

Samas and his wife Abby were supposed to be across the circle of tents from Nashu, not next to him, and Simeon had taken the move as an excuse to relocate as far away from his father as he could. Remmi, Tamarra and Fannah had finally snuck a spot next to Andrias, the burly young herdsman from up in the Nairi highlands. Seemed the move had worked out just great for everyone, Joseph mused… except… well…

He ended up outside his and mom's tent. He would have stooped to go inside except for the voices he heard through the goatskin fabric. Mom and Dad.

"Jacob, please," Rachel pleaded. "Can't we wait a few more days? Just until the baby comes?"

"Rachel, we don't have a few more days," Joseph could hear the frustration in his father's voice. "Two more days and we'll be out of water. We can't stay here."

"It's just a couple of days."

There was a pregnant pause before Jacob finally spoke again. "And what if the baby doesn't come by then?"

In the instant of silence that followed, Joseph could see Mom in his head, biting one lip, a finger idly twisting a strand of her long dark hair as she tried to work out an answer.

"Rachel, what if the baby doesn't come?" Dad insisted. "Then we have to go anyway, and we're back in the same spot, except with the baby two days closer. That's not better."

There was the sound of pacing on the floor mats inside. "It's two days to Ephrath," his father said. "There's a well there where we can water the herds. Once we're there, we'll stop until the baby comes. I promise.

In the silence that followed Joseph found himself holding his breath, until–

"Alright," Mom said reluctantly. "Two days."

***

They were nearly out of the Jebus valley now, the settlement perched like an eagle up on the low hill to the west. That meant they were close, a few hours from Ephrath. After nearly a week of moving, stopping… running, they were down to the last stretch.

No matter how fast Joseph tried to move though, the best he could do was keep up with a herd of lowing cattle in front of him. Eventually, the beating heat from the midday sun started to get to him and he fell out of the column, leaving the sheep with Asher while he dropped back to find a drink.

152

They kept several camels spaced throughout the train, each loaded down with more than a dozen heavy waterskins strapped to their saddles. On a cloudless day like today, it was about the busiest spot in their sprawling caravan. Grabbing a waterskin, Joseph walked along for a while, gulping down several deep draughts.

Catching sight of his mom seated up on a bumping camel a little ways back, he slowed his pace to let her catch up. It was odd seeing her up there at all. Camels were notoriously horrid rides, violently lurching at each step.

Normally she would have walked along with him to lend a hand with the sheep. It seemed being a shepherd was the sort of thing that never really wore off. Even now, when she didn't have to, she still went to watch the sheep now and then.

From the way he'd heard her talk over the years, she'd had a fantastic time when she'd been younger. Sometimes Joseph wondered how she and Dad could be so alike, enjoy working with the animals so much, and he'd ended up so… different.

Anyway, today Mom was stuck on the camel, Althea's orders. She wasn't supposed to *exert* herself. As she drew alongside, he could read her face screwed up in displeasure. She looked like she'd been dealing with servants in a scorching tent all day and just wanted to go outside.

"Hey, Mom."

"Joseph?" His mom glanced down at him, distracted, and it was only when he saw her up close that he realized something might be wrong.

For some reason the only thing he could think to say was, "Did you want some water?"

"I um…" Her voice trailed off and for a second, she just gazed past him, a faraway look in her eyes. Then her face creased like she'd eaten something to make her stomach cramp, and her breaths came short and shallow. "I'm good," she managed through gritted teeth.

A moment later, whatever it was seemed to pass. She exhaled a deep breath, relaxing a little, even as her delicate figure still jolted at each plodding step of the camel.

"Are you alright, Mom?"

She forced a half-hearted smile. "I'm fine, Joseph."

Joseph eyed her a second, skeptical, and tried to think what to do. "I can get Althea if it's something with–"

"It's nothing," she cut him off sharply, a stubborn determination on her face like she was willing everything to be okay.

Joseph knew that look, knew it wasn't worth arguing, and knew that things were very definitely *not* okay.

He let the matter drop, mumbled something about getting back to his sheep and jogged off.

Five minutes later he found Myrrha and her mom. In a caravan as strung out as theirs, it was easy to lose track of people. Fortunately, they were trooping along with a half dozen other servants further behind, leading trains of pack camels and donkeys. Myrrha had ended up with a particularly stubborn group of baying asses.

It had been almost a week since they'd last talked, not very long in the grand scheme of it all. But when he caught a glimpse of her distinctive yellow and white embroidered shawl, he still felt a lump like hard bronze in his throat. Especially given how their last conversation had ended, her stalking off in a fury with Amaleigh.

It felt like a lifetime since they'd last spoken. With everything that had happened, maybe in a way, it had been. Any other day his head would have been a mess trying to figure out what he could say, how to bridge the gap he felt floating between them. But today, urgency pushed aside his reservations.

"Joseph?" Myrrha looked up in surprise as he hurried over, weaving his way right in front of a camel.

"Something's wrong with Mom."

Apparently, that wasn't at all what Myrrha had expected. She glanced over to her own mother, unsure.

"Is she hurting?" Althea's face turned serious.

"Uhhh… maybe?" Joseph had no idea how he was supposed to know.

Thankfully she seemed to understand his confusion. "Come on, Myrrha." Althea handed off the camel train she was leading and gestured for her daughter to follow. "Where's Rachel?"

He found Mom still on her camel, her face screwed up with that same wincing but determined look from earlier.

She nearly jumped when Althea spoke. "Rachel, is everything alright?"

When Mom looked over, Joseph was stunned to see her blinking back tears. "It's nothing, Althea," she managed between short breaths.

The midwife arched her eyebrows, staring right through the lie. "You're having contractions?"

"Nothing out of the normal." His mom pulled a deep breath as whatever it was passed.

"How far between them?"

"A while," Rachel said, "maybe a quarter hour."

"How many have you had?"

Mom didn't answer, that determined look back on her face. "It's nothing. We'll be in Ephrath soon, and then we can–"

"Mom," Myrrha interrupted, nudging her. "Look." She pointed to a spreading stain of dark wetness creeping down the fabric of Rachel's leg.

Althea's face instantly turned grim, her voice dropping to a serious command. "Joseph, go tell your father we need to stop. Right now."

"What do you mean?" He caught Althea's worry but didn't understand.

"The baby's coming," the midwife said.

"Now?"

"Yes *now*," Althea's voice was sharp like a knife. "Go."

Joseph took off. The last thing he heard was Althea's frustrated voice, "Rachel, why didn't you say something?"

Chapter 21
Child of the Fallen

It was amazing how fast people could work when they had to. Normally the servants would have taken half the morning to unpack, put up a tent and get the floor mats laid out, but not today. Today a dozen servants had a tent pitched in no time flat. Joseph ran back from telling his dad what was happening, just in time to see Althea hurry his mom inside. Meanwhile, Myrrha quickly began hauling in all the… stuff she'd been frantically unpacking. Apparently, it was important.

Then the tent flap dropped closed, and Mom was gone.

Suddenly Joseph didn't know what to do. He wasn't about to go back to moving his sheep. Already, the herdsmen and animals had gone on ahead, making for the well at Ephrath. That just left himself, a mess of pack animals and a cluster of lingering servants standing around the tent.

The news of what was happening must have spread like wildfire, because he hadn't been waiting long when Leah strode up. She acknowledged him with barely a nod and swept aside the tent flap like she owned the place. A part of Joseph bristled. He didn't know why they were letting *her* in there. When *he'd* asked to see Mom, Althea had given a flat no.

Joseph found a spot sitting with his back to a sycamore tree. He stared at the tent flap until a voice behind nearly made him jump. "Joseph, how is she?"

His head twisted to see Dad had come up behind him with barely a sound. "I don't know," he managed. "They won't let me in."

A part of him hoped Dad might stroll over to the tent and use his clout to force their way inside. But instead he seemed to accept things stoically. "That's about the way it always is. The ladies get prickly if you try to get involved."

Joseph had a hard time understanding how Dad could be so relaxed. For his part, his stomach was churning like he'd just stripped a lemon tree bare and forced them all down in a single sitting. Then again, Dad had been here before, hadn't he? Perhaps, after a while you really did get used to anything.

After a moment's quiet, where he could just make out Althea's voice within the tent but not her words, Joseph finally asked, "So, what do we do?"

Dad settled down, his back to the nearby tree. "Not much we can do, besides wait."

For a while he seemed content to do exactly that, at least until Leah swept back outside, and spotted him almost instantly. "Jacob." Her voice was sharp, tense, which for her wasn't entirely unusual.

For a few heartbeats Joseph thought she might just share some news. But then she, quite deliberately, gestured his dad out of earshot for a short whisper-conference.

Great.

After a few moments his dad paced back over. "She's fine," he said before Joseph could ask, "Everything's... normal."

Normal? Not exactly the same thing as *fine*, given the situation. Still, Dad seemed calm enough. With nothing else to do, Joseph settled back in the patchy shade of the sycamore as the noon sun blazed overhead, and prayed that everything really was, *fine*.

Joseph started awake to a pained moan from the tent. The sound jolted his eyes open to find the world shrouded in dusk. A few steps away he saw Dad, pacing. Anxious.

"Dad? What's happening?"

Another groan rolled out from the tent and a knot of worry knitted itself together in his chest.

"It's just taking a bit longer," Dad said, putting on an unconcerned expression, even as he kept up his quick pacing.

More noises, voices from inside the tent, but Joseph tried to tune them out. Standing to pace some himself, he wandered off. Not away from the tent exactly, just far enough so he didn't have to listen to his mom in pain. It felt wrong, hearing her like that.

He glanced west and was surprised to notice the sun dropping toward the horizon. The last he remembered it had been mid-afternoon, hot, even in the shade. He must have been asleep, three, maybe four hours? He hadn't realized how tired he was.

He stared back at the tent, dark brown goat-hide with a tan linen dust curtain peeking out from behind the flap. Had they really been in there since noon?

For a long time he waited, just out of earshot. Maybe it *would* be a baby brother, he allowed himself a moment's hope. A sister would be okay, but… he really wanted a brother. It'd be nice to have someone who was his friend, no matter what. No having to worry if he should take Dan's side vs Judah's, and what that meant for later on. None of that. Just… someone who was unambiguously on his side. He'd like that. Even the thought brought a little wash of calm over him.

He'd be a good brother too. No nasty tricks like Reuben and Simeon played. No forcing his baby brother to go do work just because he was feeling lazy. He wouldn't do that, Joseph promised himself. He'd be better than that.

He was still imagining the possibilities when a
piercing scream tore the air, and his eyes flashed back
to the tent. A thousand nightmares stabbed at his mind
as his mom's wail faded

It was an effort just keeping himself to a jog.
Everything was fine, he kept telling himself, everything
was fine, everything was fine. He didn't need to run.

From the look on Dad's face though, he wasn't so
sure.

"Dad," Joseph swallowed, "is that… normal?"

For a moment, Dad didn't answer. Another agonized
scream split the cool evening, almost angry this time.
"Leah was always pretty quiet," he finally said,
subdued. "Zilpah had a hard time with Asher, but when
your mom had you it…" His face creased. "It wasn't
like that."

Dad put a reassuring hand on his shoulder.
"Regardless, that means it's almost over."

From inside the tent Joseph caught Althea's voice,
soothing tones, mingled with the occasional sharp
command.

Another shriek tore the air, louder, angrier than the
rest, until…

It stopped

For a heartbeat Joseph's heart stopped with it, then
he heard a different sort of screaming from the tent, the
high-pitched wails of a baby. Dad gave a relieved sigh,
a smile finding its way to his face. "Come on, Joseph.
Let's go meet your new sibling."

Leah met them at the entrance to the tent, breathing
hard, her hands and smock smeared with blood and
looking bone tired. "You can go on in." She swept aside
the tent flap, and Joseph walked in on a scene of
absolute chaos. Althea was cradling the baby, while
Myrrha knelt at his mom's feet, elbow deep in bloody
linens. "Mom… Mom it's not stopping." Her voice bled
frantic worry as they entered.

“What?” Joseph’s mom looked like she’d been to Sheol and back, her tan birthing tunic smeared with crimson streaks and drenched in sweat. Even so, she tried to lift her head. “What is it?”

“It’s alright,” Althea gave her a gentle smile. “Don’t be afraid, for you have another son.”

She gently lowered the baby wrapped in a blanket of linen into Rachel’s arms, before kneeling down to see what had Myrrha so concerned.

For a moment none of that mattered. Joseph and his dad both knelt next to her, and for a wonderful instant his mom’s face glowed with a smile, tears of joy in her eyes as the three of them stared at his new baby brother.

“Rachel, he’s beautiful,” Dad finally said, even as the baby gazed back, wide eyed at the three unfamiliar faces.

Joseph couldn’t stop grinning as he put his pointer finger in the baby’s hand, feeling the tiny grip latch around it.

Then, from between his mom’s legs, Althea spoke, her voice strained with urgency, and their one perfect moment faded. “Rachel, this is going to feel strange, but I need you to hold still.”

“Huh?” Mom mumbled.

Joseph glanced over to see, Myrrha, kneeling, covered in blood and… panicked.

“Leah!” Althea raised her voice to be heard outside, “Leah, Get more rags! Myrrha, calm down.” Althea looked her daughter right in the eye, before guiding her hands to a spot on Mom’s belly, mostly shrunken back to its normal size. “I need you to rub with a medium pressure here, when I tell you. Understand?”

Myrrha nodded, numbly. Althea reached down between his mom’s legs and a moment later… “Now”

Whatever it was didn’t work though. “Again,” Althea said.

They tried twice more, before Althea exhaled with a mumbled curse, "*Zû.*" Myrrha looked up, helpless tears brimming in her eyes.

"What is it?" Jacob asked.

"She's bleeding." Althea wiped an arm across her forehead, leaving a streak of scarlet, "Too much, it's supposed to stop but…"

Althea worked another frantic moment, even as Leah re-appeared with several fresh linens. "What is…?" her voice died as she saw the blood, and her face turned ashen.

Althea stood to grab the rags. "Leah, pour her whatever's left of the basil tea."

Leah swallowed audibly, but hurried over to where a little clay pot kept warm above a bed of dying coals. She hastily emptied the dregs into a cup. "Rachel, drink this."

Rachel took a sip of the tea, but even with the chaos all around her she barely seemed to mind, like her whole world had narrowed down to just the infant in her arms. Joseph found himself staring at Myrrha, kneeling there, her tunic smeared with blood, holding a crimson stained rag in one hand and almost hyperventilating, paralyzed.

"She's going to be okay? Right?"

Althea's only answer was to keep working, and Myrrha just gave a tiny terrified shake of her head.

No.

"Myrrha," Althea's sharp voice cut the air, "Myrrha, keep rubbing."

Joseph glanced back to his mom, still holding the baby, half oblivious to it all. "Mom? Are you…"

He didn't know what to say and ended up glancing over at Dad, only to see the worry creasing his face too.

"Rachel," Leah knelt next to them, breathless, "Rachel, look at me."

Slow, reluctant, Mom tore her gaze away from the tiny person in her arms and gave a deep sigh. "How bad is it?"

Leah, glanced to Althea and Myrrha, who were still trying to stop the bleeding and doing little besides staining more rags. She didn't answer, except to blink back tears. Mom seemed to understand. "Not good then," she whispered.

"Rachel," Dad took her hand in a grip that made her wince, "we'll… we'll figure out–"

"I love you, Jacob," Mom interrupted, her voice faint as she drew in an exhausted breath. "You know that, right?"

Joseph saw his dad nod, a mist in his eyes as he whispered, "I love you too."

Rachel managed a weak smile and her gaze drifted across to Joseph, who suddenly had no idea what to say. "Mom?" his voice came out, scared and small. It had always been the two of them. Mom and him against the world. Except now she was leaving too, and he was going to be alone, and…

Joseph pressed his eyes shut so she wouldn't see the tears. But he couldn't stop the sob that sent a shudder through his body.

"Joseph," his mom's voice was strangely reassuring, all those times he'd been scared and she'd told him it would be okay, rolled up together. "It's alright."

He shook his head and couldn't bring himself to look at her, his lips pressed tight together, and barely able to catch his breath. "You have to be strong," Mom said, "for your brother. He'll need you."

No. No. He didn't want this. He couldn't do this. He wanted Mom back.

He wanted to wake up and smell when she got up early to cook oat-porridge with cinnamon and honey. He wanted to help her clean out the tent, because she'd decided they had too many baskets piled in the corners.

He… he wanted to hear her say goodnight, one last time.

Joseph let out a sob and a tear trickled down his cheek. "Mom… you can't…"

He opened his eyes to see her watching him, serious faced. "Promise me you'll look after him."

Joseph didn't want to, he wasn't ready, he didn't know how and… and yet in the end, he gave a tiny nod, yes.

Mom let out a relieved sigh, like he'd taken at least a little of the worry. "Leah, you'll look after–"

"I will," Leah said instantly.

It was strange how, after everything Joseph had seen between them, the two could still understand each other with just a few words.

"I'll look after both of them," Leah added, adamant.

"Don't let Reuben and Simeon be too nasty to them."

Leah nodded, her face drawn tight against the tears. "Of course." She paused, "I… I'm sorry it's been like this."

"It's alright," Mom managed a smile, "I haven't been the best sister either. But… look after them."

For a moment, Mom just lay there, staring into the eyes of the infant on her chest, who, for his part, seemed perfectly happy to stare right back. Like he knew he wouldn't have her for long either.

Finally, Dad spoke up in a shaky voice. "What are you going to name him?"

For a moment, Rachel didn't answer. "How about Ben-Oni," she said.

An odd name, *son of my trouble*, but no one objected.

Joseph glanced over, hoping Althea had worked some miracle of her own and everything would somehow be alright. Instead he saw Myrrha, her clothes covered in blood, sobbing. Althea was sitting there, ashen faced, seemingly not sure what else she could do.

It finally sank in. This was it. Mom was still gazing at little Ben-Oni, but Joseph couldn't keep back the tears. He clutched at her wrist, and she offered him one soft smile. Then her eyes slipped shut. For a few moments her chest rose, and fell like the beat of a terrible drum, until at last it rose halfway, fell… and didn't rise again.

Sitting across from him, Dad just looked… frozen. Leah was in tears, and Ben-Oni picked that moment to start wailing, a high-pitched scream that seemed to tear at Joseph's chest.

For a minute he stared at his mother, lying there. Until suddenly he couldn't take it. He got up and just ran. He knew he was supposed to stay, be there and take care of his little brother and…

He couldn't do it.

Outside the sky was dark. The last tendrils of light had slipped below the hills to the west, and the moon was high in the sky, bathing the world in silver.

Trying to catch his breath, Joseph stumbled off into the night. Not sure where he was going, just… Mom was gone.

He stumbled to a stop a way off. Most of the caravan had moved on. It was just their tent and a low dying fire that he could look back to see. He halted at the trunk of a tall oak and sank down, his back to the rough bark.

It was cold and dark and he… didn't care. He just he wanted mom back. The tears came rolling down his cheeks.

He didn't know how long he sat there, knees curled to his chest. Finally he heard a shout through the dark. "Joseph!" Myrrha's voice. Her shout hung in the air a second before, "Joseph! Where are you!" There were tears in her voice too.

He didn't answer.

"Joseph!" She tried one last time, and far off he could see her silhouetted against the fire, staring out into the night. The desperation in her shout cut at him, "Come back! Please!"

He didn't though, not yet. He wanted to be alone.

Myrrha finally retreated back into the tent. For a long time Joseph sat there, alone, watching as the stars carved circles in the night sky above.

Chapter 22
Faded Starlight

Joseph wasn't sure how long he sat shivering outside. Eventually though, the sharp night breeze forced him back to the tent. Everyone was already asleep when he returned, Mom's figure covered by a linen sheet that stood out, even in the dark of night.

Finding a spot in the corner, he curled up under a blanket and tried to think what he would do now, until at last sleep took him.

He woke to find the first brush of dawn outside. His dad was just getting up, brushing aside the tent flap. Althea and Leah were both gone, and some ways off he could hear the soft crying of Ben-Oni amid the first morning chirps of birds.

That left just him and Myrrha, on opposite sides of the tent. He was exhausted, but with all the thoughts racing in his head, Joseph doubted he could sleep. Eventually he sat up, curled beneath his blanket, staring at the shroud that covered Mom's body.

Across from him Myrrha stirred, her eyes inching open to see him. "You're back."

It wasn't a question, but Joseph nodded.

For a little while both of them sat there in silence until Myrrha let out a miserable sigh. "I'm sorry," she said with a defeated expression. "Last night, I didn't know what to do and I…"

"It's not your fault," Joseph said numbly.

"Still… your mother was a good woman and…" she blinked a few times, rubbing at her eyes. "I'm sorry."

She meant it different the second time, and Joseph gave a small nod. Not sure what else there was to say really.

After another few heartbeats, Myrrha pushed off her blanket and rose to leave. She'd changed out of her scarlet smeared tunic from the night before, replacing it with a simple white one that fit her slight figure.

Stooping to leave, she looked back. "Do you want something to eat?"

He almost said no, a part of him feeling like it wouldn't be appropriate to eat after… everything. But the mention of food seemed to remind his stomach of just how hungry he was. After a heartbeat staring at his mom's shrouded figure, he tore his eyes away to meet hers. "I suppose."

Myrrha disappeared outside, and a moment later Joseph stood to follow.

The brightening glow above the eastern hills slowly spread across the sky, as Myrrha found a stick and poked around in the coals from the night before. It took a while, but eventually she uncovered a glowing ember and added a few bits of dry grass and sticks to coax the flames back to life.

One of the camel trains was still close by. Someone had tied them up to several nearby trees, where they'd promptly sat down, legs folded beneath them like a pack of oversized, smelly cats. Grabbing a clay pot from the baggage, she added some water, a hefty helping of oats and just a pinch of salt, before wedging it down in the fresh coals. She set to stirring it for a while. Oatmeal, her usual recipe… well, almost. Normally she added too much salt, or, as she called it, 'a good portion'. Today though, she'd left it a bit light, a small thing, but scooping out some into a bowl and handing it to him, Joseph appreciated the gesture.

A little ways off came the steady scrape of a shovel in loamy dirt. His dad, digging.

For a while Joseph picked at his porridge, trying to ignore the sound, and eventually Leah and Althea returned. Leah had little Ben-Oni draped on her shoulder, bouncing him a hair with each step and humming a soothing tune in his ear.

He'd stopped his crying, and taking a seat near the fire, Leah took him in her arms. "Do you want to hold your brother, Joseph?"

He wasn't sure. He didn't know what he was supposed to do with a baby, but she was already offering the swaddled infant over to him. Ben-Oni was surprisingly light. Wrapped up tight in a linen cloth, he was a warm, chubby-faced bundle.

"You have to support his head," Leah leaned over to show him. "You can't let it roll back, or it can hurt his neck. That's why you want to hold him on your shoulder or with your arms, so that–"

"*Okay*, I get it," Joseph snapped. It came out harsher than he'd meant, but he didn't really want a lecture on the art of baby handling.

Holding his little brother in the crook of his arm, Joseph stared at him for a moment, a pair of perfect brown eyes looking back. What was it like, he wondered, to not know? To have no clue what had happened to Mom? To think everything was still… fine?

Eventually Dad returned, sweaty and breathing hard, wooden spade in hand. He slid down next to them with barely a word.

For a minute Joseph wasn't sure what to say. Finally, Myrrha broke the glassy quiet with a simple bowl of breakfast. "Would you like some porridge, sir?"

His dad nodded, and for a little while he busied himself eating. At last though, he gave a deep sigh, and stood. "Joseph, I'll need your help with…" his voice faltered for a beat, "with your mother."

Joseph's heart froze in his chest at the words. "Do we have to? Now?"

Returning, his dad had looked so calm and collected, but now the shell cracked for an instant. Joseph caught a glimpse of the cyclone of grief raging inside as dad struggled for an answer. "We have to."

A part of Joseph felt like it seized up at the words, and for a second he could barely move. He knew Dad was right, but he hadn't even said goodbye, and now they had to bury mom and…

"Can I have a minute?" He brushed at his eyes.

Dad just nodded.

Wandering back into the tent, Joseph stared for a time at the shroud, before pulling it back to uncover Mom's face. She was pale now, but her last peaceful expression still lingered, and the sight brought more tears to his eyes.

If there was one thing he'd learned living with his brothers, it was don't cry. Ever. Even when you got hit, and it hurt, and you had to limp the whole next day. Don't cry. It was the sort of mistake you only made once.

Now though, alone in the tent, he stared at his mom, her face trapped in death. He felt the tears coming and for once didn't try to stop them. "I'll try and take care of Ben-Oni," he promised her in a halting whisper. "And I… I love you, Mom."

He found her hand, cold now, but it was the last bit of her he had to hold on to. Kneeling there, alone, Joseph wept.

***

There was something horribly undignified about burying someone. Watching a life reduced to a body

170

laying in a hole in the ground. Myrrha had told him once that, in her homeland, they burned the dead in great pyres of flame and smoke. At the time he'd thought it sounded absurd, but helping Dad lower his mom's body into the grave, he started to see the appeal.

He didn't watch as Dad scooped the first shovel of dirt over her. He didn't want his last memory of her to be… that. He only looked back when the hole was half full of dirt, the shroud vanished beneath.

When they were done, Dad set up a rock pile atop the grave and said a few words. It all seemed wholly inadequate. Standing there, Joseph felt like he was living in a dream, the world drifting by around him. And yet, as much as he was certain the day could never go on, because Mom wasn't there with him, slowly, it did.

Afterwards they took down the simple tent, packed it onto the camels, and set out again, making to catch up with the rest of the camp a couple of hours away in Ephrath.

Through it all, Ben-Oni behaved surprisingly well, like he somehow understood just how serious it all was and kept quiet. It wasn't until they got moving that he started to get antsy. Joseph had taken to carrying him, and now the baby was making little whimpering sounds.

Falling back a few paces next to Myrrha, Joseph asked, "Do you think he's okay? He seems kind of upset and…"

"He's probably just hungry," Leah interrupted from up ahead. Joseph's lips drew tight with a stab of irritation, as she dropped back and calmly took it upon herself to scoop the squirming bundle out of his arms. He hadn't been asking her.

"We gave him a little water and some mush this morning," Leah continued, holding his baby brother up so he was face to face with her, her voice transforming to a gooey baby talk. "But a little mush isn't nearly enough for you, is it, Ben-Oni?"

"We're not calling him that," Dad cut in.

"What do you mean?" Leah laid Ben-Oni on her shoulder and went to patting his back, which he seemed to enjoy.

"Ben-Oni," Dad said, "I know it's what Rachel said, but he's not growing up with a name like that. Always a reminder of what happened. It's not fair to him."

Joseph saw his point, kind of agreed with it. For a minute Leah strolled along in silence, like she was thinking through it all. "What do you want to call him then?" she finally asked.

Dad must had been thinking about it for a while, because he had a new name ready, "Benjamin."

Benjamin, *son of my right hand*. A good name, Joseph thought. Leah considered it a few heartbeats before agreeing. "Alright then," she kept patting him on the back as she walked, "Benjamin."

Chapter 23
Benjamin

Two days later, Joseph ducked out of Mom's – *his* tent. He waited a second, before breathing a long sigh of relief when he didn't hear any high-pitched wails from inside. He hadn't realized just how *needy* babies could be. Not being able to say what they wanted didn't make it easier, you just had to guess. Were they cold, hot, messy, tired, hungry, or just unhappy for no reason at all?

Well, at least for a few hours Benjamin would be asleep. That helped.

It was late afternoon and already Joseph could smell the aroma of dinner clouding the camp. Hurrying over, he found himself near the front of the line for the oversized bronze pot of soup Dhra had been simmering all afternoon. You never quite knew what you were going to get with Dhra's soup. Sometimes he was feeling *inventive,* and his taste buds seemed a little different from everyone else, especially when it came to spices. At least once, Dhra had made his soup mouth-scorchingly inedible for the rest of them, even as he'd cheerfully scarfed it down.

Tonight though, it was a good flavor, just enough spice in the broth. Joseph found himself with a bowl full of tender, fall-off-the-bone goose, mixed with chickpeas and a nice touch of oregano.

The lamb skewers weren't quite done yet, so he beat the usual line and managed to barely miss the crowd. Wandering over to a nearby oak, he dropped down cross-legged in the shade, appreciating the moment's peace as he watched the rest of the camp starting to line up for the meal.

That was, until Leah walked over. From the instant he made eye contact, Joseph already could guess it was going to be bad. He could tell from the way she walked, like she was tensed for something.

Past two days, Leah had seemingly made it her personal mission to butt into his life. A part of him harbored the hope she might just be wandering through and ignore him, right until she sat down four feet away. No such luck.

"You got Benjamin down to sleep?"

No, he'd just abandoned his baby brother out in the middle of nowhere. Joseph sighed, "Yeah."

"He didn't make too much of a fuss?"

He'd made a horrible fuss actually, a good twenty-minute tantrum about… nothing. But Joseph wasn't about to give her any excuse to step in and snatch back the tiny bit of control he had with his brother. It had been hard enough getting her to trust him with Benjamin at all. "He did fine."

"And what about you?"

"I… put him to bed?"

"Not that," Leah sighed. "Joseph, after what happened, it's normal to be upset. Your father won't show it because he–" Her voice cut off there, like she was straying into something private. "My point is, if you need to talk, my tent's always open to listen. It… it helps."

Did it? Joseph wasn't so sure. It felt an awful lot like she was just trying to *be* Mom. All of a sudden, fifteen years of problems were brushed under the rug, and she was his best friend. All because Mom was gone, she felt guilty, and was trying to make it up.

Joseph swallowed back a stab of anger. He didn't want to be Leah's charity project. He'd gotten enough of those looks when they'd arrived at Ephrath a few days earlier, everyone cheerful to see the new baby, right until they'd realized that Rachel wasn't there.

"Won't bring Mom back," he muttered, his tone acrid.

He caught the stab of hurt on her face, but for once didn't care.

"She was my sister too," Leah's voice stiffened a little. "Joseph, I know what it's like to lose her."

No, Joseph had to bite back the storm of words in his throat. She didn't know. Not at all. Because she still had half a dozen children who'd fight tooth and nail for her, she had Dinah, and Dad, and more or less ran the camp when she was in the mood.

He'd had *Mom*, and that was all.

Now he didn't even have her, and just to rub salt in the wound, he had to go kowtow to Leah for something as simple as making sure Benjamin didn't starve.

He was pretty sure she had no idea. How could she? She wasn't alone.

He doubted she would understand, and he didn't see the point in making her angry. "I need to go check on Benjamin," he said, with the last shreds of politeness he had left.

Grabbing his stew, Joseph stood to leave with Leah's pleas following, "Joseph please, just–"

He didn't hear the rest.

Didn't matter.

With dinner in full swing, Dhra was busily ladling out his stew and proudly accepting compliments. The center of camp was a mess of hungry people returning for seconds. Joseph skirted around the edge of it all. It meant going the long way, but at least he got to avoid everyone.

He found a spot back at the entrance of his tent and had just about finished off the stew, when even more people he didn't want to see showed up. Specifically, his brothers.

"Hey, Joseph," Levi said in an attempt at a friendly voice. He wandered up with Issachar, Zebulun, Gad and Asher all in tow, most of Levi's oddball entourage looking unusually self-conscious. "How are you doing?"

Joseph nearly retorted, 'Better, before you showed up' but pushed that away in favor of a sullen, "I manage. What do you want, Levi?"

Levi took a seat a few feet away, and for a moment, couldn't quite force the words to come out. "I – *we*, wanted to tell you we're really sorry about what happened to your mom."

"Bit late for that." Joseph snapped, his pent-up frustration from earlier finally spilling out.

Levi sighed. "I know we should have said something earlier. I meant to, just…"

His voice trailed off as Joseph stared at him in utter disbelief. Was he actually this blind?

"What?" Levi asked.

It wasn't worth it, Joseph repeated over and over in his head. It wasn't worth it. Levi was just an unobservant idiot and it…

"Just, please go away."

"Joseph," he said frustrated, "we're just trying to say we're sorry, okay. Why can't you–"

"NO! You're not." Joseph slammed back in his face in a fury. "Because if you *were* sorry, you wouldn't have caused all this. You wouldn't have left a string of ruined people across the countryside. You wouldn't have murdered a whole cursed city. We wouldn't have had to run, and Mom wouldn't be buried back there on the side of the road. Are you here to apologize for that, Levi?"

"Joseph, I…" For an instant Levi was lost for words. "I didn't know any of this would–"

"Good thing you never let that stop you," Joseph muttered.

"I was trying to save Dinah."

"Well, I'm glad you got what you wanted, and everyone else be cursed. Seemed it worked out just perfect."

Inside the tent Joseph heard a noise he'd come to dread in the last few days, a high wail, rising to an unhappy scream. Benjamin.

"*Zû.*" The curse slipped out almost on its own, and Joseph stood to go get his little brother, casting a last glance at Levi. "Just, go away, you've already ruined enough."

For an instant Levi sat there, looking lost. Joseph ducked into the tent, and the last thing he heard was Levi's quiet, "I'm sorry," trailing him.

When Joseph reappeared outside, trying to calm his little brother, his other brothers were gone.

He'd learned little Benji seemed to like going on walks. He wasn't sure why, but for once Joseph didn't mind. Taking his little brother, he wandered away from the camp, the short grass that carpeted the ground brushing at his ankles. Climbing up one of the rolling hills that seemed to go on almost forever, with Benjamin's implacable wails right in his ears, he glanced back. The little village of Ephrath was visible, sitting at the crest of the next hill over. It had caused quite a stir, their showing up in force outside the unwalled town, with rumors of death and God and light from the clouds darting on ahead of them.

They seemed to have reached a truce of sorts though, at least for a little while. Everyone putting up with everyone else until they moved on.

It was ironic, Joseph thought. The last week they'd been constantly moving, forced from one spot to the next. But now they were here, stuck in a place where no one wanted them, and they didn't really want to be either, and yet they were staying, at least for a while. Maybe they all just needed a break.

Wandering up the steep hillside, past the scrub trees that grew more and more the further south they went, Joseph finally stopped at a large rock. Benjamin's screams grated at his already vanished patience. Patting the little boy on the back, he found himself desperately pleading with the infant. "It's okay, Benji. Just go to sleep, please."

It didn't work and the baby just shouted more. He tried patting him on the back, which didn't help at all. There was only so much screaming he could take in a day though and finally his patience snapped. "SHUT UP!" he screamed back, "Just, shut up! Please!"

He felt horrible, shouting at a baby. He knew he shouldn't just… he didn't know what else to do. Not that it helped.

He was already on the verge of frustrated tears, when a girl's voice interrupted behind him. "Joseph, are you okay?"

He turned to see Myrrha, ten paces away, staring at him, witness to everything. He could have pretended, said it was fine. If it had been his brothers he would have, but in that instant, he was too miserable to try and hide it. "No." His head dropped as the helpless tears came. Tears for how no one understood, for how impossible dealing with Benji was, for how much he hated going to sleep every night in a lonely tent. For how he could feel what little he had left starting to slip away. Tears because Mom was gone.

He felt Myrrha's hand on his shoulder. "Here, let me take him."

He surrendered his still screaming brother. Myrrha took him and began humming softly as she rocked him back and forth. Somehow the little guy went absolutely silent. Finally, Joseph could breathe again. A part of him knew he should stop sobbing, not make a fool of himself, but… it was Myrrha.

"It sucks," she said after a moment. Something of a general statement.

"Yeah," Joseph barely managed.

She leaned up against him, and a little ember of calm seemed to radiate out from where their shoulders met. Something strangely reassuring about just touching another person.

"I just wish things could go back to the way they were," Joseph said. "I know they weren't perfect but…"

Myrrha nodded.

"Everyone's trying to be nice. *Oh, poor Joseph*," he said, mocking. "Suddenly everyone wants to be friends, and it's all just so…"

"Pretend?" Myrrha supplied.

"Yeah," he drew in a halting breath. "Something like that. I just wish it hadn't taken Mom being gone to change things. What sort of a world is that?"

She nodded. "I'm sorry she's gone," Myrrha added, staring down at Benji. "I always liked your mother. She was kind, even when she didn't have to be."

For a little while they sat there, the sun dropping lower and painting the clouds to the west in streaks of purple and scarlet.

Finally, Benji let out another little cry, like he was finished waiting.

Joseph wiped at his eyes and sniffed back his tears. "I don't know what he wants."

Down in Myrrha's arms, Benji was grabbing at her chest. She gave a little grin. "I think he's hungry."

Joseph hesitated, "You're a girl, could you uh…?"

She apparently got his jist, because her grin widened, amused. Myrrha shook her head. "Doesn't work that way."

Joseph sighed, but Myrrha didn't seem terribly worried, instead her voice transformed to a cheerful baby-talk. "We need to get you food, don't we, little Benjamin?"

She poked at his belly, and looked back at Joseph. "I think Leah's been having Abby feed him. She was just weaning Nathanial anyway, so I don't think she minds."

Myrrha hesitated a heartbeat. "We can go ask if you want. She and Samas are set up right next to Mom and I anyway."

"Yeah." He gave a slow nod but didn't move. There was still one thing that had been hanging like a cloud between them, and he just wanted to be rid of it. "I'm sorry," Joseph added.

"Huh?

"When I got back from Shechem, the whole slave thing… I'm sorry. I wasn't…"

His voice trailed off, but Myrrha seemed to understand. "It's alright," she shrugged, "you weren't wrong, just… it was a really awful day and I…"

She couldn't quite complete the thought either, but somehow they both seemed to understand. Things were okay, at least between them.

Standing, Myrrha laid Benji over her shoulder. "Come on," she said with a warm smile. "I think he'll be alright once Abby can feed him. All the rest we can figure out together."

Yeah, Joseph forced himself to his feet, a spark of reassurance in his chest. Together.

That could work.

TO BE CONTINUED

Afterword

Thank you for reading *The Days of Joseph*. If you enjoyed this dramatization of Joseph's story and want to help share it with others, I encourage you to leave a review on Goodreads and Amazon. Reviews help others discover the story and contribute to the continuing success of the book. If you're reading on a Kindle that can be as easy as flipping on through to the end.

If you're eager for more of Joseph's story, you can check out the next book in the series here: *The Days of Joseph Book 2: The Lost Brother*. In the meantime, I've written a short story covering Joseph's adventures years before this book, when his family first returned to the land of Caanan. You can check it out here: *The Days of Joseph – Mahanaim*.

If you want more full length Biblical Historical Fiction, then I'd encourage you to explore my other book, *The Days of Elijah*. And if you're into science fiction, I have a series you can check out that starts with *Medea*.

If you'd like to receive email notifications when I release new books, you can head over to my website Jnoblewrites.com, click on New Releases and sign up for email notifications.

Finally, if you'd like to reach out to me personally, you can email me at johntheauthor1@gmail.com.

When I began writing a story about Joseph, I usually got surprised looks when I mentioned where I was starting. When my little sister Rachel found out what I was up too, she asked about his coat of many colors, and I told her I was writing the story before that one.

Conventionally speaking, the story of Joseph begins in Genesis 37:2. It starts with the stories everyone is familiar with, Joseph's coat of many colors and his dreams. But I've always felt that focus short-changes Joseph, because in reality his story didn't just *start* there. He had a life before the coat of many colors. He had experiences and friends and enemies and passions and desires that certainly colored the decisions he made afterwards. Similarly, his brothers didn't just decide they hated him one day. Family problems like that might manifest in a moment of anger, but the roots typically go back a lifetime.

To be honest, that idea of exploring a story never told posed more than a little challenge. Partly because the Biblical narrative is amazingly detailed in some parts but has gaps big enough to drive a battleship through in others. Inevitably there is a great deal of filling in the blanks, and that's always controversial. You can see that even in how God is depicted. In the original text it's not really explained how God shows up at all the two times he does speak with Jacob. So I've filled in that blank with my own vision of the God from Job and Elijah, who showed up in a thunderstorm and a pillar of fire. But, then there's the God of Abraham, who walked up to Abraham's tent and shared a meal with him. Truthfully, I don't know if I'm wrong or right, all I can say is I've tried to tell the story in a way that makes sense to me. That's the best I can do.

The other issue is that the original story of these events in Genesis 34 doesn't really focus on Joseph at all. It's more about Jacob finishing his own journey home and receiving God's promise. Part of the reason I wrote the story from Joseph's perspective is because I really think the events surrounding Genesis 34-35 must have influenced him very deeply. How could they have not? But that rarely gets mentioned, because Joseph doesn't get an explicit byline in the text.

And yet Joseph's whole life was changed because of a few rash decisions made by Shechem, Simeon and Levi. I've always wondered how that must have felt, and I've always had a great deal of sympathy for Joseph. He probably had an extremely difficult childhood, which wasn't made any easier by the events here.

That said, I've tried to incorporate what we do know from the Bible, and hopefully I've captured the spirit of the story. Just like the Days of Elijah, I've included the direct dialogue from the story. And yes, I'm aware ancient Hebrew doesn't have quotation marks and dialogue was routinely paraphrased when written. It's just how I decided to write it.

Also, as you've likely noticed, I've added in a lot of characters along the way to paint in the world around Joseph. Perhaps the most humorous case being Althea, who I originally made up as the camp midwife, before realizing that she actually got an explicit line in Genesis 35:17 and thus wasn't really so completely made up.

I've tried to keep these characters at least plausible although my imagination did run a little wild at places, and Jacob's camp developed into something of a motley trans-national crew. If you didn't already puzzle it out, Dhra is from somewhere in India. Which isn't as wild as you might first think, given that Bronze Age trade networks spanned from tin mines in the modern United Kingdom to at least the Indian Subcontinent. Nashu is a Minoan from Crete (Kaphtor being the name used at the time). Samas is from Lagash in modern Iraq, basically the New York City of its day. While Myrrha and her mom are, of course, early Athenians from Attica in Greece.

As a side note, this book does stray onto the issue of slavery, which always an uncomfortable topic, but sadly a reality for millions of people throughout history. We don't know a huge amount about slavery in the ancient Levant except that it happened, frequently. Commonly it might occur as a result of war or unpaid debts, and people's experiences in servitude likely varied dramatically based on their particular circumstances. It's been an interesting balance, trying to treat the topic with the seriousness it deserves, while also writing about a world where it's a fact of life no different than the passing of the seasons.

I'll also briefly mention a few questions my Mom raised when she first read through the story, in case anyone else was wondering. Shovels, which feature several appearances, likely existed at this time and probably would have been carved wooden spades or possibly animal bones, the broad scapula being a popular choice. Coins, on the other hand, don't seem to have existed before the 7th century BC, and Herodotus records that their first usage was among Greeks living in Lydia (modern day western Turkey). In Joseph's day, trade and payment would have been conducted either through old fashioned barter, or by weighing out bits of precious metals on a set of scales. Hence the importance of having honest weights and scales.

Another common question is the environment. Historical Shechem would have been a small walled settlement whose footprint is still visible today. It's located near the modern town of Nablus in the West Bank. If you've ever been there, you might have noticed the lush tree-capped mountains of Joseph's time no longer exist. That's largely because, since Joseph's time, this part of the world has been fought over and occasionally razed to the ground, by the Canaanites, Israelites, Assyrians, Babylonians, Egyptians, Persians, Macedonians, Ptolemies, Seleucids, Romans, Parthians, and Sassanids. And that's just through the fall of the Western Roman Empire. Since a common part of warfare has historically involved devastating the countryside, each army marching through has left its own trail of ecological destruction which has accumulated to the present day. An excellent example of this style of ecological warfare is found in 2 Kings 3:25, if you're interested.

At the same time, evidence seems to suggest that the middle east in general has been growing cooler and dryer over the last several thousand years. The prodigious forests Solomon cut to build the first temple are gone, withering as the area has gradually dried out. We can't say exactly what Canaan was like during Joseph's day, but it was likely much lusher and closer to the land flowing with milk and honey described in Exodus than it is today.

This leads to another point of minor interest. Camels. Camels are believed to have been domesticated as far back as 3000-2500 BC, hundreds of years before Joseph. They likely would have been common in Mesopotamia in Joseph's day. However, based on bones excavated from rubbish piles, it's currently believed that domestic camels were not introduced to Israel until around the time of David and Solomon.

That said, Abraham is mentioned as having camels in his own travels. I've taken the view that, since Abraham and his family were originally from the city of Ur in Mesopotamia, they likely would have brought some from there. His grandson Jacob would have been familiar with the creatures and probably acquired some of his own in Harran which was a major trading hub of the time. Regardless, despite their availability, they don't seem to have caught on in Canaan for nearly a thousand years, possibly due to the wetter climate making them unnecessary.

The last thing that seems to consistently surprise people is the portrayal of Joseph as a teenager. Most people have this image of him during the events of Genesis 34 as a young boy. Unfortunately, the best I can do is to point out that this view is neither wrong nor right, because we simply don't know. Joseph is a kind of Schrodinger's Child; he is potentially many different ages at this time.

What we do know is this: Joseph was born sometime during Jacob's stay in Harran. When Jacob returned to Canaan, Joseph was a young boy of uncertain age, and by the time we get to the coat of many colors, he was seventeen. This leaves a lot of wiggle room.

Dinah offers a bit of help resolving this issue. We know she was born last of Leah's children and seems to have been close to Joseph in age. If we assume she was abducted by Shechem sometime from age 13-18, which feels reasonable, then Joseph would plausibly have been anywhere from a young teenager to the fifteen-year old portrayed in this book. In my personal chronology, the book is intended to take place 10 years after Jacob returned from Harran and 2 years before the coat of many colors episode.

I'll wrap up my historical ramblings by simply saying that, regardless of whether Myrrha, Amaleigh, Nashu, Samas or many others actually existed in history, I hope you enjoyed the story and took away something helpful from it. I know I learned a lot on my adventure writing it.

I'd also like to thank my whole family, Mom, Dad and my three sisters who have been very encouraging along this journey. When I first published the Days of Elijah, I knew that the journey to become a writer was a long one. I didn't know that the journey *after* becoming a writer is just as long and filled with different but no less treacherous pitfalls. So, thank you to my family for being there, as well as to everyone else along the way who has read my books and offered reviews or even emailed me. As an author it's a very unique and special privilege to know that someone you've never met enjoys your work.

Lastly, one of the things that amazed me writing both the story of Joseph and the saga of Elijah is just how crazy it all is, in a good way. Some of the plot twists along the way really caught me by surprise, even when I was writing them. I don't plan my books so my stories surprise me more than you might expect. I know… shameful.

Regardless, things happened that I never would have dreamed up on my own. More than a few times, I found myself at a point in the story where I thought, *Wow, I can't believe that just happened. That's crazy.*

It's a cool feeling, I hope you shared it, and I'll wrap up by saying that we all owe much thanks to the Lord God for coming up with a fascinating and wonderful adventure.

And for your convenience, here are all the references from earlier:

The next Days of Joseph Book – The Lost Brother

A Days of Joseph Short Story – The Days of Joseph – Mahanaim

My other Biblical Historical fiction story – The Days of Elijah

My Science Fiction story – Medea

Get New Release Notifications -
https://www.jnoblewrites.com/new-releases.html

My email - johntheauthor1@gmail.com

Citations

Ancient Hebrew doesn't have quotation marks, and dialogue was routinely paraphrased. That said, I used exact dialogue from the Book of Genesis where translators provided it. I mixed and matched Bible versions to find the translation I felt flowed best within the rest of the narrative. Below are the biblical references for the book. The Chapter in *this book* where the citation is used is listed first and the biblical chapter and verse numbers are listed second. The appropriate version citations are shown last. If you have ten minutes, I'd encourage you to check out the source material as it's pretty readily available. Note: full verses are often cited but only the dialogue is actually quoted.

1. Chapter 5: Genesis 34:8-10 (NIV)
2. Chapter 5: Genesis 34:11-12 (GNT)
3. Chapter 6: Genesis 34:21-23 (NLT)
4. Chapter 11: Genesis 34:30 (NLT)
5. Chapter 13: Genesis 35:2-3 (HCSB)
6. Chapter 15: Genesis 31:32 (HCSB)
7. Chapter 17: Genesis 35:10-12 (NIV)
8. Chapter 17: Genesis 35:17-18 (HCSB)